Burial

Robbie Dorman

For The Sleepytime Bandits.

1

Emma walked down the road, leading her horse. She couldn't ride here, not with the state of the pavement. The horse would turn an ankle, and that wouldn't do, not with how far she had to ride. The pavement would be gone in a few miles again. She'd saddle up then. For now, she'd walk the horse.

The wind rustled the trees as she walked. It'd been a long time since she'd been this way. They'd gone back to the City by carriage, and it had traveled a different route. Emma hadn't been this way since—

—before you met James. You were still flying solo. Hadn't even rowdied up the gang yet—

"When are we stopping next?"

The voice brought her out of her thoughts. She didn't

answer.

"Stop ignoring me. I'm tired. I want to rest."

"You shut your mouth," said Emma. The wind rustled the trees again. It was dead silent otherwise, not even the sound of wildlife. Hunters probably cleared out anything worth eating long ago. This far from the City, anything was fair game. Even her.

"I will do no such thing. I'm tired of being treated like this—"

"Shut your goddamn mouth," said Emma. "You can go on being tired, because nothing is going to change."

"Is that right? After all we went through, you're going to treat me like this. Ole Cass is spinning in his grave right now, seeing how you're treating a blood brother."

"Ole Cass never got buried," said Emma. "He got eaten by vultures, what little left of him there was. The Mongers chopped him up good."

"Those sons of bitches."

"He killed Smith's brother. What did he expect to happen? I've got no love for the Mongers—"

Memories of James floated through her mind, and it cut her off.

"That ole cuss was only doing what was expected of him."

Emma sighed. "Are you going to talk like this the whole way? I should cut out your tong—"

She heard the click of the rifle and knew it was already too late. A voice yelled out from around her.

"Freeze. Keep your hands where we can see 'em. Give us everything you got and we'll let you live."

Emma froze for the moment. The voice was coming from her left, and slightly up. The thinning forest that surrounded her gave them safe cover, but the voice could only be coming from behind the big boulder up ahead of her, maybe 30 feet. Probably perched on the top, just out of sight. That's where she would have sat. Gotten a good vantage point.

"Who's we? Got a mouse in your pocket?" she yelled back.

"Don't you worry, there's a good number of us," said the voice, deep and torn, a voice like a rock pile. "Throw down your weapon."

"No," said Emma. She stood there, next to her horse. Listening. She let the sounds around her come to her, like she always had. Her eyes and ears weren't as sharp as they once had been, she couldn't help her age, but she still saw and heard more than most men ever would. Sounds came to her. The rustling of the wind through the leaves, for sure, but others as well. Breath, trying to be held shallow. Fingers rubbing against leather. A gun cocking, the click of oiled metal on metal.

"Fine," said the voice, and he poked his head out, the barrel of a rifle leading the way. She couldn't see his face, only the silhouette of his hat and the barrel. As he did, a dozen others popped out from around trees, and around the base of the boulder the leader laid down on top of.

Emma scanned them all quickly. Only a few had guns and most had only a blade. Not a well keeled group. Scavengers, trying to make their way into being a gang, hoping the numbers and their rifle would do the work. Get enough of people like her, and they'd all be armed, and they could start being formidable.

But they weren't formidable yet.

"Get out. Go. Leave," said Emma. "Leave me be and I'll

forget your faces."

A silence hung there as the scavs looked her over.

"You're one woman and a horse," said the leader. "You ain't in no position to be threatening. Give up your weapon, now. Last chance, or I gun you down on the spot."

Emma didn't need to wait.

She was never the fastest draw. Not even in the top half of her old gang. Not like they ever timed it, or anything. The only contest that mattered was who survived the fight, and Emma outlived them all. She was slower now than she'd ever been. Father Time had made sure of that.

The leader had her dead to rights, already sighted in on his rifle, for sure. Same goes for the few others she saw with pistols, also near the boulder. All drawn on her, that's a couple seconds she lost. But how good of shots were they?

Emma was never the fastest draw, but she never missed. In one practiced motion, her right hand flew to her pistol hanging at her belt and she drew, aiming first at the leader with his rifle. As her hand flew, she took a step to the left. Just a single step. But it was enough.

The leader fired and missed. Emma aimed for the dark face below the brim of a shadowy hat BANG and she didn't need to look to see she hit him. She already had moved on to the next target. Both of the scav's pistols were slower than their rifle, but they had both fired by now, right after she got her shot off. The single step had thrown off their aim, and they didn't have time for more than one.

All of Emma's loss was to her draw, but now her pistol was out and she fired twice more, taking the two guns out.

BANG.

BANG.

She hadn't seen any other guns from them, but she knew they would rush her. She had three more shots and she got one off BANG before she felt something hit her legs.

Shit

One of them blindsided her from under the horse, and then the numbers game caught up to her, and they were on her. She had lost, lost to a bunch of scavs. But she wasn't a knife fighter, never had been, and she was too old to fight a bunch of hungry nobodies.

"I give," she said, loudly. Maybe they wouldn't kill her.

They pulled the pistol from her hand and yanked her hands behind her back. Someone had rope and they were tying a knot.

"We should kill her—"

"Don't you dare," said a voice, a woman. She had retrieved one of the pistols, walking over to where the rest of them were, next to Emma and her horse. Most had already abandoned Emma, giving her horse a look over, seeing what they could grab, aside from the horse itself.

"She killed Keith," said the other, a man, holding a knife. His sunken cheeks told her he was hungry.

"Yeah, she did, and now I'm in charge. And since I'm in charge, I say we don't kill her. Look at her. She came from The City. They might have a bounty on her."

"I'm not doing business with The City—"

"You shut your fucking mouth and do what you're told. City money will get us supper just like anything else. And they care if their prisoners are alive. So if you kill her, you'll be the next one dead. One less mouth to feed. You got a problem with that?"

The hungry scav eyed her with venom, but said nothing,

and walked away, investigating Emma's horse like the others. They were picking through her saddlebags. They hadn't touched the bundle on the back of the horse yet.

"You got a name?" asked the woman.

"D'you?" asked Emma.

"Yeah, Mary," she said. "I can't sell you back to The City without a name. And if I can't sell you, then I might as well kill you."

"My name's Emma," she said, meeting Mary's gaze. Her fingers were busy on the ropes knotted around her wrists. Whoever had tied them had done a shit job, and she moved quietly, working through the clumsy knots. Mary held a pistol, five shots in it. Emma's own gun was tucked in Mary's waistband, with three shots left. It was enough.

"What's in this bundle?" asked someone near the horse.

"None of your fucking business," said Emma.

Mary stared at her, pointing her revolver at her.

"I think it is our fucking business, considering it's all our property now," she said. "What's in the bundle?"

"It fucking stinks," said another voice. Emma heard them unwrap it.

"I wouldn't do that," said Emma.

"Shut up," said Mary, taking her eyes off Emma. Mistake. "What is it?"

Mary looked to the group at the horse, as they unwrapped the bundle.

"God, it reeks," said a voice. More noises as they unrolled it.

"Jesus, it's a fucking body," said another.

"What the fuck?" said another voice. "It's half rotted. Had to have been dead a few wee—"

Emma ignored them. Mary was looking at them as they investigated Billy's body, her eyes off of Emma, and the barrel of her pistol had wandered to the side. Emma had navigated the shitty knots they had tied.

"What the fuck are you doing with that body, lady—" started Mary, but Emma was already moving, testing her aging knees and hips, hoping they would follow orders. She swung out with a leg, catching Mary in the back of her knee. Mary fell, off balance, and Emma took her pistol, easy as pie, and fired once into Mary's chest as she went down BANG and she heard a deep hollow meaty thud as Mary died. Emma fired the four other bullets in the pistol BANG BANG BANG BANG, each hitting a person near her horse, all falling. She dropped the pistol, and grabbed hers from Mary's waistband, fanning as she fired the gun empty BANG BANG BANG. Three more scavs slumped.

There was one left standing, the hungry man who had wanted to kill her. He stood next to Billy's body, his eyes wide, staring at her in complete and utter shock. The scav still held his dagger, realized himself, and then dropped it. He put his hands up, and then turned and ran.

Emma stood up, her knees popping, and walked over to her horse, emptying her revolver and reloading, 1, 2, 3, 4, 5, 6. She stepped around her horse, and saw the man running into the forest. She raised her pistol and fired BANG and he fell, skidding for a few feet before stopping.

Emma emptied the one empty shell and reloaded, 1, flicking the cylinder back home and holstering her gun. The wind rustled through the trees. The horse snorted, stomping his hooves, and Emma went to him, softly petting his neck. He hadn't been born in gunfire, like most of the horses she'd ridden in her life. He'd get used to it, with time.

She sighed. This would cost them some daylight. But maybe they could still make it to Alton by dark.

The horse settled down. Emma went to Jimmy, tucking him inside his bundle, and wrapping it tight, layering the bunches of lavender that kept the smell down. She tied him back to the rear end of the horse, and made sure everything was still in her saddlebags. They hadn't taken anything.

The bodies were next. They were scavs, but maybe they had something useful. She climbed the boulder, and found a little gold on the leader. Not much, but something. It had City stamps on it. Would pay for their room and board in Alton, at least. She looked over his rifle. Not good enough for her to take, but she could sell it. Same for the two other revolvers. Nothing much else on the rest.

There were twelve dead, and she thought to stack them, but she didn't have the time. She'd leave them for the buzzards, or for any soul desperate enough to go cannibal. Doubt there were any here. Maybe farther west.

Emma led the horse, keeping her eyes up for any more problems. She worried that the gunfire would draw more trouble to her, but the rest of the road was empty, for today, at least.

The pavement ended, and she mounted the horse, easing the pain in her feet.

"Jimmy would be proud of you for that display of gunfighting back there," said the voice from behind her.

"You keep his name out of your mouth, you hear me, Billy?" asked Emma.

"Oh, I'm so sorry," said Billy. "Those stupid assholes had no idea who they were dealing with, did they? They thought they could just sneak up on you and take your shit. They didn't know they were fucking around with Emma Burns, did they? Those sorry motherfuckers."

"I thought I told you to shut your mouth," said Emma. "It's your fault they got the drop on me, anyway."

"Always blaming me for everything," said Billy. "Where's our next stop?"

"Alton," said Emma.

"It's been a while since we've been in Alton," said Billy. "We ever hit their bank?"

"They ain't got no bank," said Emma. "And I told you, stop talking."

Billy laughed. "It's all I have, Emma. You took everything else."

2

"Wow, Alton sure has changed. Positively cosmopolitan," said Billy. They had made good time after the ambush, and the sun still peeked over the horizon when they got to Alton. The lamplighter was walking around, getting ready for dark.

"Yeah, no drunks puking up their guts, or people shitting in the street," said Emma.

"Hey, I'm going to call it progress," said Billy.

"It's just The City getting closer," said Emma. "It's pushing the wildness out, farther and farther."

Alton was an old settlement, one of the oldest still standing that hadn't had The City come in and take it over. But Billy wasn't wrong. The town seemed quiet as they rode in. It wasn't big, less than a square mile, with a tavern, general store, stable, and doctor on the main drag. Used to be Alton wouldn't go more than five minutes without a fight or a shootout. A few people milled around, but that was it.

Emma rode her horse over to the stables. She didn't recognize the hand that greeted her.

"Your stables are safe, right?" she asked, dismounting.

The young hand didn't blink. "Yes, ma'am. We got twenty-four-hour lookouts." His nose wrinkled as she walked the horse to him and he took its reins. "Your animal stinks."

"It ain't the horse that smells," she said. "It going to be a problem?"

"No," said the hand.

"Don't wash her," said Emma. "You can clean her hooves, but leave that bundle be. You hear?"

"Yes, ma'am," said the hand. Emma grabbed a pack off the side of the horse, and the hand led it away.

"You're just going to leave me out with the horses all night?" asked Billy. Emma didn't answer, walking to the tavern. Lester's Tavern. He'd updated the sign. It used to be plain wood, but he'd painted it gold sometime in the meanwhile. It also served as an inn. Emma needed a roof over her head tonight. And maybe a bath.

Lester eyed her close as she walked up to the bar. The place was mostly empty, except for a fella drinking at a table, his eyes on his beer, and a kid playing the piano in the corner. Emma didn't recognize the song.

"That you, Emma?" asked Lester. Lester had gained a little weight and lost a little more hair in the five years since Emma had seen him, but his soft voice sounded the same.

"Last time I checked," said Emma. "I need a room, Lester. And a bath drawn up."

"That'll be two, then," said Lester. Emma tossed him a fiver, one of the City stamps that the leader of the scavs had carried.

"Hold onto the extra for now," she said.

Lester nodded. "So, it's true," he said, inspecting the coin. Emma didn't answer. "My room?"

Lester stared at her for a moment, and then reached below the bar and came back with a key.

"Second room upstairs," said Lester. "Give you some privacy. The boy will get you a bath going." He yelled across the room, to the kid at the piano. "Bart, customer needs a bath."

The kid ended the piece of the song with a short flourish on the instrument, and then ran out back.

"Bath still in the same place?" asked Emma.

Lester nodded. Emma returned it and went upstairs to her room. It was small, but the bed was soft, and there weren't any windows. Emma threw her pack on the bed and took off her boots. She dumped out spare bits of dirt to the side. She gave the boy a few minutes to heat her up some water, and then she stepped out to the bathroom, on the other end of the second floor.

Emma found the boy dumping a few buckets into a big tub. The boy was probably ten, and meekly smiled at her as she came in. He finished emptying the buckets and then stacked them, leaving the room. She waited for him to leave and then locked the door behind him. Don't know if there'd be other customers tonight, but she didn't give a shit. She didn't want to be interrupted.

She undressed and lowered herself into the hot water. It stung at first, but she didn't slow as she sunk into the bath. A little extra water surged over the side and splashed onto the floor. She dunked her head, her hastily cut graying hair soaking up the water. She ran her hand through it, pushing the dust off into the tub. It had been a few weeks since her last bath. A fews weeks since she'd left. A thousand thoughts tumbled through her mind and she dunked her head again, pushing them away.

She didn't have time for that shit.

Emma came back up and washed herself, grabbing the bar of soap next to her holster. She didn't expect any trouble, but that didn't mean some wouldn't find her. She focused on the task, banishing any intrusive thoughts. Thoughts about her mission, about Billy. Thoughts about James.

She pushed them away. She couldn't push them away forever, but she didn't feel like tackling them now. The hot water eased her aching joints as she finished, dried off, and got dressed in the change of clothes she had brought in. She hung her holster back on her belt and returned to her room. She could hear a soft buzz coming from downstairs. A few more people had shown up, and the young boy played the piano again. She recognized the music. A song to dance to. Emma liked the song, even if she never danced.

She looked in the mirror in her room, pulling her hat back on. She still didn't recognize herself with short hair. A part of her wanted to sleep now, and hit the road early in the morning. But the other half desperately craved a drink, and some conversation with somebody that wasn't dead. Plus, Lester kept his ears open. He might have some useful info for her.

The piano player had switched to another song when Emma arrived downstairs a few minutes later. She sidled up to the bar, sitting as alone as she could manage. A few tables were occupied now, and a gentleman and a lady sat at the other end of the bar, engaged in conversation.

"The usual?" asked Lester, walking over to her.

"If you remember it," said Emma.

"How could I forget?" asked Lester. "You're the only person with money I know who would drink the swill." He reached for a green bottle with a deer on the label and poured her a glass of the brown liquid.

"What can I say, I like the taste," said Emma.

"You're lucky I have any left," said Lester. "They're having trouble finding more."

"They'll have to scavenge somewhere else," said Emma. "The old world will only give up so much."

"Won't matter anyway," said Lester. "The City will take this place soon enough." He paused. "*Is* it true?"

Emma eyed him. "What did you hear?"

Lester glanced around, even if it was clear there was no one within earshot. "That you and James went City. That you sold out the gang."

"Don't believe everything you hear," said Emma.

Lester considered her. "Then where you been? Where's James?"

"I said don't believe everything, Lester. I didn't say you were wrong."

Lester sighed. "You haven't changed much, I'll give you that. Won't say a word you don't have to."

"Don't hurt my feelings, Lester."

"Oh yeah, all those feelings you got. You go City and all of a sudden you've got feelings."

Emma took another sip of her drink. "I'm not City. We *were* there, but I'm not going back."

"What about James?"

"What about him?" asked Emma.

"I don't see him."

Emma took another sip. "We had a difference of opinion," said Emma. "He wanted to stay. I wanted to go. So I went."

"Somehow I don't believe that. That man would have died for you a hundred times."

"Don't believe everything you hear."

"Somebody told me that, once," said Lester. "People don't leave The City. Not once they've gone in."

"You gonna rat on me?"

"Course not," said Lester. "I'd never do such a thing. If I were a rat, they woulda found me hanging from the roof of the bar long ago. Or shot, out back. Squealing ain't no way to stay alive. You're gonna hurt *my* feelings, you keep at it."

"I don't want to hurt you, Lester," said Emma. "I just want information."

"Oh yeah?" asked Lester. "What kind?"

"Alton has changed," said Emma. "What happened? Normally, by this time of night, there'd already been two bar brawls and maybe a gun fight. But neither of them has happened."

"The wildness went farther west," said Lester. "Scared off by The City and their rangers. Enough hot shits thought they could take them on, and they mostly wound up dead. Gangs wised up and left. Desperate ones might come in, range for a day or two, and then fuck off again, but mostly they stay out in The Frontier."

"Who's out there?"

Lester thought for a second. "Mostly the same as before

you left. Mongers, duking it out with The Gloves. Most of the smaller gangs either took a knee, or went out into The Scraps. God knows what found them there. What I hear is that it'll only be The Mongers soon. They've taken that stronghold, and they're in there like a tick."

"They got the stronghold," said Emma. "Fucking hell." She finished her drink. "Another, please."

"I'm glad you're drinking this," said Lester. "Otherwise I'd have to pour it out for the dog." He refilled her glass.

"Anything else you hear?" asked Emma.

"I hear you've got wolves on your tail," said Lester.

"Which ones?"

"A ranger came in the other day," said Lester. "I assumed they were looking for a stray Monger. But now you show up—"

"I'm not afraid of a ranger," said Emma. Lester eyed her again, and raised an eyebrow.

"You sure?" said Lester. "That fella looked hard. Holloway."

"He gave you his name?"

"I have my ways," said Lester, smiling. "And I heard something else. But then again—you can't trust everything you hear—"

"What did you hear, Lester?"

"Agatha," said Lester. "I heard Agatha was around. I didn't think much of it. Figured her and Billy were sitting fat and happy—" He trailed off as he studied Emma's face.

"Fuck me," said Emma, quietly into her drink.

"So she is looking for you," said Lester. "What happened to Billy?"

Emma stared at him for a moment and said nothing,

taking a drink.

"You killed him, didn't you?" asked Lester. Emma didn't answer.

She drew her revolver and fired BANG one shot, and Billy slumped over. She took no chances, and fired again BANG into his head.

"What happened, Emma?" asked Lester, his voice low. "Why did you and James leave?"

"Mind your own business, Lester," said Emma, finally, her voice hardening.

Lester breathed deep. "Let me know if you want another drink." He walked off, checking on his other customers. The boy still played the piano, and switched to an old world song, one that Emma knew. They'd sing it with the boys at camp, back when they were young. It was sweet, and catchy, and it hurt to hear it.

Emma finished the rest of her glass and retreated upstairs. The walls of her room kept out the song, and the buzz, and she only had to compete with the thoughts inside her head, and not anything from without. She could handle those. She'd dealt with them her whole life, and she could keep going.

Another week of hard travel would get her there. She could deal with them for a week.

She stripped and laid down in the soft bed, her door locked and her pistol on the bedside table. Her weariness overwhelmed her regrets and fears and she fell asleep quickly.

It was the bed that did it. It was soft, and comfortable, just like their bed back in The City. Sleeping on the ground hadn't reminded her of him, but the bed did.

So she woke up in the middle of the night, reaching for James, reaching for his familiar presence, knowing that together they could defeat anything.

She reached for him and she was alone and she questioned everything.

3

Emma was up before the sunrise. The taste of liquorice dwelled in the back of her throat from the drink the night before, and she guzzled some water before the aftertaste made her vomit.

Lester was still awake downstairs when she dropped off the key.

"Sleep okay?" he asked, polishing a glass. The bar was empty.

"As good as I'm able," said Emma.

"You've got some change coming to you," he said.

"Keep it," said Emma. "I'm sure you'll find use for it. Take care, Lester."

Emma went to leave. Lester stopped her.

"Emma—" he started. She glanced back. "Whatever

you're up to, be careful. The world ain't what it used to be."

"I know," said Emma. She left.

She shouldered her pack and looked to the horizon, orange blooming, hints of the sun. She went to the stable and retrieved her horse, paying the hand that got him. Everything was as she left it.

She stopped at the general store, just opening. Emma sold off the spare guns, stocked up on rations, and filled up her canteens.

"You got any rad pills?" she asked the shopkeep. He looked at her askew.

"I haven't seen those in a long, long time," said the shopkeep. "You're not going to the wastes, are you?"

Emma didn't answer his question. She took her extra gold and left, the shopkeep eyeing her. Back on her horse, and a few minutes later, Alton was behind her.

"Left me out in that horse stall all night," said Billy, as soon as they passed the city limits. "It stank like shit."

"*You* smell like shit," said Emma. "Reminds me." She stopped the horse and grabbed a bunch more lavender as they passed it on the road, stuffing it into the bundle.

"Ain't gonna do anything, Emma," said Billy. "You know that. Ain't nothing gonna hide the smell now."

"I'm not tryna to hide it. Just trying to soften it."

They rode some more, the path long and winding, the pavement long cracked and fallen apart. Emma looked to the ruins as they passed, mindful of any more ambushes. The only other presence there were some birds. The trees had reclaimed much of the rubble.

"Why are we heading to the wastes, Emma?" asked Billy's voice, out of the blue.

"You know why," said Emma.

"It's a fools errand," said Billy. "It's an old wives tale. Superstition. It's all nonsense."

Emma paused. "You believe it, though, don't ya?"

Billy didn't answer.

"That's what I thought," said Emma. "That's all that matters."

"Can't get there anyway," said Billy. "What are you going to do? Fight through all the Mongers and the Gloves?"

"I've got no trouble with the Gloves," said Emma.

"Yeah, but the Mongers are still run by Trevor," said Billy. "You think he's forgotten what we all did to him?"

"*We* didn't do anything to him," said Emma. "You did. You stole from him and acted like I told you to."

"You kept your share," said Billy. "You and James both."

"Trevor already thought us guilty," said Emma. "Might as well take the gold for it if it's all the same in the end. I can get through The Frontier. No matter which gang we run into. It won't change anything. They'll let me through."

"And after that?" asked Billy. "The Scraps, The Remnants—"

"The Remnants are empty," said Emma. "Aside from the dregs. And I'm not afraid of them."

"You've still got the ranger to worry about," said Billy. "And Agatha—"

"Lester was talking out of his ass," said Emma. "He was fishing for information, to use as bait for the next person who sat at his bar. Alton is about to get et up by The City, and he's spending his last days gossiping about rangers. And when was the last time you even saw Agatha?"

A brief pause. "Same time you last saw her."

"And you think she's going to come for you?" asked Emma. "Her leaving wasn't amicable. I was there."

"Doesn't matter," said Billy. "We said the oath, and we never broke that. Nothing happened between us changed it."

"Maybe in your mind," said Emma. "But not in hers. If she's out here, if there is a ranger after us, where are they?"

Emma looked around, listened. Nothing but birds, and the rustling of the wind through trees. No galloping hooves, no human breath, no footsteps. Nothing.

"No one cares, Billy. No one is after just the two of us. There's more pressing matters for The City, for Agatha. No one gives a shit."

"What about James?"

Emma didn't answer, only kept her eyes forward on the road, even as her guts turned to acid.

"You know he's coming after you, Emma. He won't let you go without a fight."

Emma took a breath. "He's already lost it."

"You don't know—"

Gunfire interrupted Billy's voice, up ahead, and Emma took the horse off the road, through the brush, and tied him to a tree, far back into the forest, behind a ruined building. Enough cover to be safe. She sneaked up, picking her way through the underbrush. More gunfire from up ahead, louder now as she approached. She kept her head down. Catching stray fire from a gunfight was no way to die.

A clearing was up ahead, and she saw the source of the strife. The Mongers and the Gloves, fighting it out. They were on opposite sides of a creek, ducked behind rocks and trees. Any cover would do in a battle. They fired back and forth. A couple bodies lay on the ground, dead or dying. One lay face down in the creek, the small current trying to pull it downstream. She saw a Monger vest, and yep, there were the trademark leather gloves of the Gloves.

Emma watched as they fought. The worst had already happened, and the Mongers had the numbers game won, as they spread out and pressed their advantage, flanking the Gloves on Emma's side of the creek. She laid on her belly, in the brush, and covered herself with leaves, while the gunfire still hid all her noise.

The Mongers set down covering fire as members of the gang advanced, and then they were on top of the few Gloves left, pinned down in a shallow ditch, doing all they could not to get headshot. They were only thirty feet away, and their conversation drifted over to Emma.

"Come out and throw down your weapons, or you die here," said a Monger. "Your choice."

A beat passed and then two pistols and a rifle came flying out of the ditch, followed by a voice. "That's all the weapons we got. We're coming out. Don't shoot." The pair emerged, dirty and dusty. One cradled a gunshot wound to the side, a thin trickle of blood dripping down his pants leg.

The Mongers moved them to the creek bank and surrounded them. The rest of the gang joined them. One of the Mongers stepped out, the leader of this squad.

"Which one of you is senior?" he asked, looking between the two Gloves, both on their knees, hands behind their heads.

"I am," said the one not injured.

"That was easy," said the Monger leader, and he shot the other in the head, point blank. He fell over, dead, and the remaining Glove stared at him with rage.

"Get up," he said. "Let's take you back to Trevor. He can decide what to do with you."

They bound the last Glove's hands with rope and walked him away. Emma heard horse hooves in the distance ahead of her. She waited a few minutes longer, and then, confident they were gone, went to the fallen bodies in the clearing around the creek. She rooted around in their pockets, pulling everything the Mongers had left behind.

Trevor's let them get sloppy. She would have reamed anyone who had left guns and ammo behind.

She didn't recognize any of the bodies, and then returned to her horse.

"What the hell happened up there?" asked Billy.

"Mongers fighting with the Gloves," said Emma. "Mongers won. Took a Glove prisoner. Taking him to Trevor." Emma talked as she stowed all of her loot, putting everything in its particular place.

"Don't you want to follow them?" asked Billy, as Emma carefully put everything away. "You're going to lose them."

"I already know where they're going," said Emma. "And with the way they were moving through the country, there's no way I could miss their tracks." She mounted the horse and went, following the path the Mongers took. She kept her pace slow, slower than she would like, but she didn't want to run into them, not out here.

They had seemed to be moving quickly, and their destination was nearby, but Emma was careful anyway. Their steps weren't hard to follow. They led directly to the stronghold Lester had mentioned. Emma slowed as she approached, taking the horse off the path.

"Where are we headed?" asked Billy. "Thought we were following the Mongers."

"Do you ever shut up?" asked Emma, as she took the horse up a slight incline that weaved back and forth until they were on top of a small hill. She dismounted and tied the horse to a sapling. It'd do. She didn't want to be seen until she wanted to be seen.

Emma climbed further up, scrambling up a few steeper inclines until she was on top of the hill. If she remembered correctly, it looked out over the stronghold. It was quiet as she lowered herself to her belly on the gravel, and slowly crawled out to the edge of the cliff.

She was right. The little hill overlooked the fort, and she saw down into the mammoth structure.

The fort had a lot of names over time, depending on who occupied it. It had never interested Emma. She had always preferred they stayed mobile, and the amount of men need-ed to hold the area was restrictive. And the fact that the place had traded hands so many times over the years had proved her right. She didn't want to play warlord. She just wanted gold.

At first, at least.

But she could see it clearly now, and whoever had it over the past five years had built it up. They had filled the holes in the walls with stone and mortar. The three watchtowers had all been repaired, too. Either Trevor had done it or taken it from someone who had. She assumed the former, but you never knew.

She pulled the glass from her pouch and put it to her eye, extending it out. There was always the risk of someone seeing a reflection, but she wanted to see what she was getting into. The Mongers had expanded, it seems, with dozens of men inside. She tracked the group that had captured the Glove, following them as they moved through the compound. They stopped, and she saw him. Trevor stepped out from a tent and sized up the Glove. They disappeared inside. Interrogation next. And then torture if they didn't give the answers Trevor wanted. She doubted Trevor had softened in these five years.

She looked out past the fort. The land beyond it was flat, and the stronghold itself was elevated, giving all the towers good line of sight over anything.

Could they sneak by? Maybe. If they waited until night and were quiet. If she rode hard through the dark, she could be out of their territory.

But she didn't like her odds. If she knew Trevor, and looking at the number of men they had, they'd have rings of patrols, and she'd have to sneak by every single one. And if they caught her trying to slip by, they wouldn't give her any slack. They'd kill her.

Better to play it safe. Or safer, at least. None of this was safe. The possibility of safe had disappeared quite some time ago.

Emma put away the glass and slithered back and stood up, returning to her horse, who hadn't moved. Neither had Billy.

"What's the story, morning glory?" he asked.

Emma didn't answer, mounting her horse and taking it back down to the road. She dismounted there and walked the animal forward.

"What are we doing? Don't tell me we're going to see Trevor," said Billy, his voice urgent.

Emma walked down the path, and soon it opened up, and she saw the fort, its front gate dead ahead. She held her hands above her head then, still holding the reins in one.

It didn't surprise Emma when a voice yelled "Halt!" from on top of the gates. She cast a glance up at the figures guarding the entrance.

"I'm here to see Trevor. I want to parlay."

<h1 style="text-align:center">4</h1>

"This is a bad idea," said Billy, but Emma ignored him, walking forward, keeping her hands up, in plain sight.

"I told you to stop," said the man again, trying to sound hard. Emma looked at the sound of the voice, stopped where she wanted to be, and repeated herself.

"I'm here to see Trevor. I want to parlay."

"I don't give a shit if you want to see Trevor or not. Who the fuck are you? Why shouldn't I gun you down on the spot?" The voice yelled at her, and Emma saw the crown of his head peek out from above her. The barrel of a rifle was visible.

"Tell him Emma is here to talk. I want safe passage."

"Emma? Who the fuck do you think you—"

The other figure cut him off. "Shut the fuck up, Harold. You are the world's biggest fucking idiot. That's Emma Burns. You're lucky she hasn't turned your head into a canoe. Lucky she hasn't turned both of our heads into a canoe—"

"How the fuck am I supposed to know—"

"One moment, Mrs. Burns. We'll be right back with you."

Both the figures disappeared, and Emma lowered her hands.

"Trevor only bringing on the best and brightest," said Billy.

Emma said nothing, only waiting and listening. A few minutes passed, and the guards returned. Someone opened the gate below, a heavy block of wood being moved, and the iron gate swinging open. Two Mongers stood there. Emma lifted her hands above her head once again.

"That's not necessary," said the one. He was short and wide, with a thick, bushy beard, black as raven. "Trevor said you're to be trusted."

Did he now?

Emma questioned that, but said nothing, leading her horse inside the compound. The second man, blond and plain-faced, followed behind as the bearded man led her deeper inside.

"I'll take you to him," said the bearded Monger, and Emma followed. She'd never been inside the fort. Had been by the stronghold dozens of times, sometimes sneaking by in the dead of night, and sometimes allowed to pass through precarious truces or treaties. But the fort was from the old world, and then rebuilt, and destroyed, and rebuilt again. She didn't know how old it was. Men lingered around, some doing melee combat drills, others smoking rolled cigarettes.

Everyone glanced at her. Emma studied the faces of the men as they passed.

They were so young. She had known the Mongers before they went to The City. They were never close with them, her and James and Billy and everyone else, but they knew them. They knew Trevor. But these men were young rabble, cobbled together by Trevor. And only men. No women in The Mongers. Not as official members, anyway.

She wasn't surprised the guard at the door hadn't heard of her, much like none of these young men had heard of her. Five years was an eternity out here. Life was measured in days, not years. All these men had grown to adulthood by luck and meanness, and they assumed the same of everyone else.

Emma followed through the various groups of gathered Mongers, past the outbuildings and the cleared spaces where there once had been ruins, to the back of the fort, where the oldest buildings still stood, sheltered by the cliff face it was built against. Emma spotted the repairs. The bearded monger showed her to a door, opened it, and gestured inside. She handed him the reins of her horse.

"It's worth more than your life," she said, simply, and then walked in without a response. He shut the door behind her.

She found herself inside a cement room, with a huge woven rug on the floor, a metal desk near the back of the room. Trevor Smith sat behind it. The room held a chill, but Trevor wore only a thin white shirt and his Monger vest, no different from the one worn by all other members. He wore blue jeans and leather boots. Expensive.

He looked at her as she entered. He was alone.

"Hello, Trevor," said Emma.

"Emma, Emma, Emma," said Trevor, smiling. "Please, come, sit." He gestured to a chair in front of the desk. A metal folding chair. Salvaged from the old world, and worth more than the lives of half the men in the fort. She sat in it, testing it. It creaked slightly, but held.

She stared at Trevor. He was a little older than her, his greased back hair all white, his face full of stubble. His eyes were dark, his slim mouth grinning.

"I did not expect you at my doorstep, of all people," said Trevor. "Asking to parlay. Didn't want to sneak around, did you?"

"I did the math," said Emma.

"You always were smart that way," said Trevor. "Where's James?"

"I don't know."

Trevor stared at her. "You're not lying. What do you want from me, Emma?"

"I want safe passage," said Emma. "That's it."

He stared at her for a beat. "Why did you leave The City?"

"You don't need to know that."

"It's part of the cost of giving you safe passage," said Trevor. "Information is valuable. It's why I'm still alive."

She sniffed, and stared back at Trevor. He would smell a lie. "Billy Ray Brunner's body is on my horse. I'm taking him to the Wasteland."

Trevor raised his eyebrows. "You're taking Billy out there? He was an idiot from time to time, but nothing he ever did deserved that. And to leave The City for it? Is that why I heard Agatha is down here again? She coming for you?"

"I don't know," said Emma. "Maybe. Doesn't change anything."

"Sure as hell does," said Trevor. "Agatha is out there and you want me to guarantee you safe passage? I protect you, and she'll come after me next."

"Are you really worried about Agatha? She doesn't give a shit about Billy, not anymore. They had it out years ago, and I doubt they've talked since. And they sure as shit aren't gonna talk now."

"That's fair enough," said Trevor. "But there's a ranger snooping around. Did you leave The City, with the body?"

Emma stared at him for a second. "Yes."

"Fuck," said Trevor, shaking his head. "So he is after you."

"I'm not afraid of a ranger," said Emma.

"Well, I am," said Trevor. "Can one man gun us all down? Probably not. But we start shit with him, The City will be here in a second, and we *cannot* stand up to them. We can only pray that they don't want to move this direction while I still breathe. God, if they take The Frontier, what's left?"

"The Scraps, The Remnants," said Emma.

"And there ain't shit there but the dying and God knows what else," said Trevor. "I'd rather die of a gunshot than from the fucking tumors. Jesus."

"There's no ranger in this room. Agatha isn't here. I want safe passage."

Trevor held her gaze for a moment longer, and took a deep breath, rubbing the bridge of his nose and squeezing his eyes shut.

"Do you have any idea the hell I've gone through trying to get The Mongers to a place of stability?"

Emma told him the answer he wanted to hear. "No."

"No," said Trevor. "You and James fucked off to The City. Threw a match behind you and didn't look back. Don't blame you, necessarily. Thought to do it myself, more than once. But The City wouldn't want me, anyways. I can't clean myself up, not like you and Jimmy. So I tried to make a go of it out here. Thought to settle further east, but the goddamn City kept getting closer and closer. Scared the shit out of me."

"They'll take the west in ten years or so," said Emma.

"How do you know that?" asked Trevor. "You got sources inside?"

"No," said Emma. "I've got working eyes and ears. They need more land, more resources. More than that, they need control. They need their authority recognized by everyone. Otherwise, it's not real authority. You know that better than anyone."

"True enough," he said. He spat to the side. "Fucking City. But I know why you all never tried to take this damn fort. It was a bitch and a half. And the fucking Gloves have been up my ass about it. They launch raids from every damn direction. Hit my men when they're not ready."

"Probably doesn't help you're hiring children," said Emma.

Trevor stared at her for a second, and then rolled his eyes. "You're not wrong. Boys are so young we're practically teaching them to shave. But who else is there? Anyone with a brain is scrambling to the teat of The City, and all the vets are dying off or retiring."

"You could retire," said Emma.

"That's not for me," said Trevor. "Or for you, it seems."

"No," said Emma. "Not anymore."

Trevor stared at her. "I'll give you safe passage."

Emma stared back. "For what?"

"The Gloves won't stop giving me trouble," said Trevor. "I tried to make peace with them, I did." Emma thought to question it, but said nothing. Trevor continued. "They won't have it. Won't coexist with me. Don't want to share. They want it all. So I need to break their back. No more hit and runs, no more guerrilla warfare. No more losing men out in the wild. I want to stop them, for good."

"What do you want me to do?" asked Emma. She waited for the other shoe to drop.

"They have a camp, thirty or so miles north of here. Just on the border of the Wildlands. It's their headquarters. Most of their stockpiles are there, along with most of their men."

"How many men?" asked Emma.

"A few hundred," said Trevor. "Been a while since we've gotten a scout close, but doubt the number has changed much. We've hit them hard nearby, so they've kept their distance. But I doubt that sticks."

"I can't take out a few hundred men," said Emma. "I'm not invincible."

"You don't need to," said Trevor. "You need to destroy their stockpiles. Only reason most join up is to get fed. If they don't have rations, they'll spread to the wind, and they'll be done for."

Emma studied him. "You want something else."

Trevor nodded. "Taking out their stockpile should do most of the work. But I can't have them regrouping. You need to kill their leader."

"Who? Ethan?"

"No," said Trevor. "Ethan ran off a few years ago. Disappeared."

"Makes sense," said Emma. "Ethan could barely tie his shoelaces."

"Gloves were never a threat under him," said Trevor. "If I had known, I would have done all I could to keep him around. He kept them docile. No, the new leader goes by Red. Big man, shock of red hair. He's pretty smart, too. But wants control over all the west, and I can't let that be."

"He a warlord?"

"I don't trust him, Emma," said Trevor. "I can't understand him, so I don't trust him. And I need you to kill him. Kill him, take out their resources, and I'll give you safe passage."

"But you trust me?" asked Emma. "I could just nod and smile and then run."

"You could," said Trevor. "But you won't. You'll do what you need to do. That's what you are."

5

"You can't trust him," said Billy.

Emma had slept at the Monger stronghold, and was up again before dawn, on the road, heading toward the Gloves camp, where she would do what Trevor wanted. She would destroy their resources, kill their leader, get safe passage, and be on her way.

They rode north, this stretch of land empty except for scattered trees and grasslands. No sounds of birds, no sound of insects. The trees were the only thing that still lived. Made it easier to hear approaching hooves or footsteps. The sound of chatter, or gunfire.

"I can trust him fine," said Emma. "He's never done me wrong."

"Sure he has," said Billy. "He sold us out to Tyrone, back

when Tyrone was still alive."

"He didn't sell us out," said Emma. "He sold *you* out. You and Agatha, because you tried to squeeze a deal under his nose and he didn't appreciate it. I wouldn't have appreciated it either. You do low-down dirty shit, expect repercussions."

"Either way, this is a bad idea," said Billy. "You don't have to do this."

"You suddenly friends with the Gloves?" asked Emma.

"No," said Billy. "I've got no love for them."

"Then what does it matter?"

"You're not an assassin, Emma," said Billy.

"I killed a dozen people two days ago, Billy," said Emma. "I've killed countless more through the years. What's one more, if it'll get me to the Wasteland?"

Silence hung in the air.

"I don't want any more death," said Billy. "I've seen enough of it in my life."

"You don't get to tell me anything about killing."

"I didn't know, Emma, I didn't know—"

"Shut up—"

"I thought you were alone, goddamnit—"

"You shut your goddamn mouth, for once. I'm going to go take care of Trevor's problems, and then we're going to go to the Wastelands, so I can bury you where you belong."

Billy did what he was told and they rode. Emma kept to the side of the road where she could, her eyes and ears open for any approaching Gloves. Trevor had offered her an escort, but she'd rather be alone. Easier to avoid attention that way. They rode hard. She wanted to be outside the camp by nightfall, so she could sneak in, do her work, and get out.

They traveled for hours as the sun rose, the path winding. Billy kept silent, and Emma felt her mind wander. It thought to her promise to James, so long ago. The promise she had broken. She had told him, told him no promise didn't matter anymore, that the grounds for the promise had been broken, so what did it matter if—

Stop it, Emma. Ain't no use thinking about it now.

She reeled her thoughts back, kept them confined to the road in front of her, and the mission she was on. Get into the Gloves camp, do the dirty work, and get out.

They went way back with Trevor and the Mongers, back when the Mongers weren't much bigger than them, a loose assemblage of hardened men under Trevor's command. Trevor wanted to be a gang, to be a recognized power. Emma never cared much about that. They never kept people around long enough to be called a name anyways. People died, ran off. A few stuck around longer, and she could have given them a name, because they were her gang, for years. And then she met James, and it became *their* gang. But still—

The sound of hooves brought her out of her mind, rumbling down the path from ahead of her, and she took the horse off the road quickly, spotting a copse of trees with brush built around it, and she pushed the horse in, before they could come within sight.

She dismounted, and held the horse tight as she peered out through the brush.

She had expected to see Gloves, out on patrol.

Instead, she saw Agatha.

Fuck.

Emma had held out hope that the rumors were just that, rumors, and that Agatha had stayed up north, where The

City still didn't reach. Emma had always kept away from the North, but if you could handle the cold, there were still ruins ripe for picking, and plenty of places to raid. Agatha had left them years back, back when she and Billy finally had it out, and Billy was the only reason Agatha had ever bothered sticking with them at all. Emma always fought with her, over her pushing the envelope. If a little bit of pain inflicted would get Agatha even a half a gold more, she would do it without thinking. Emma, and then James, held her back, kept her worst tendencies in check. But she stuck around for Billy. He made her laugh, when no one else did, and that went a ways with Agatha. But she caught him fucking around on her, and that was it. She was gone.

But Emma knew Agatha loved Billy. She had to have, because she didn't kill him.

Emma watched as she rode past, with a dozen other men, furs strapped to their bags, pulled off and stowed as they came south. These weren't lightly armed scavs. These were hard men and women, all of them carrying long guns, with pistols at their waist. Agatha rode second, her scout ahead of her on a light horse.

Agatha herself was deadly with all weapons, a good shot, fast, but could handle herself in a knife fight, or with any thrown weapon. She was a killer, and every single person in her band was a killer, too. If Emma tried to fight them on open ground, she would die.

There was no doubt in Emma's mind why she was here, down so far south. She was after Emma.

Emma watched them pass. She had kept the horse off any soft dirt and moved back and forth, hoping it would be enough to cover their tracks. Old habits, never broken. If they noticed her marks, they said nothing, only continuing onward.

She held still, keeping her breath silent, holding the horse close to her. They had cover, and were a ways off the road, but Agatha's instincts were sharp and dangerous. Emma waited as they passed, riding back the way Emma had come, toward the Mongers camp.

She gave them ten minutes, until their hooves were long distant, and there was no sign of them returning.

Emma mounted her horse, and rode back to the road, and continued on her way toward the Gloves.

"I told you she would come," said Billy. "She always did love me."

"You fucked that up," said Emma. "Like you fucked up everything."

He was silent, and they rode. The horse was strong, and they made good time, only stopping to rest a couple times. Emma's stomach growled as they neared the Gloves camp. Trevor had said it was near where the rivers met, and they were close. She could wait to eat until the deed was done. Her hunger would sharpen her mind.

The sun was setting as they approached where the camp should be. Emma went off the road again, the trees clustered tightly, and tied off her horse, leaving it and Billy behind as she scouted ahead. There were no hills here, no vantage points to spy. She'd have to get close. She saw the encampment before long, as she sneaked through the underbrush, keeping her head down and her body behind cover.

These are the men terrorizing Trevor?

The camp looked thrown together, with scattershot fencing thrown up in places, but not in others. A half dozen tents stood in the clearing behind the wooden enclosure, different colors and cloth. The river was behind them, clear why they chose this spot. But also they could never hold it against an organized force. Men loitered around a couple campfires, softly talking. She didn't see any supplies. She'd have to get closer.

Emma crept in as close as she would dare in the waning light. She waited as the sun set, and the camp lit torches around the perimeter. Not many, only enough. The two campfires provided most of the light.

Their defenses were light. A few lookouts, but no towers, and the guards leaned on their rifles. Emma stayed down and quiet, no matter how much her knees and back ached, and circled the encampment, getting a count on their men. Just over twenty visible, with probably more in tents. A large canopy tent stood at the back of the camp, with a dual complement of guards at the front. The leader had to be there. Two other larger tents stood back there as well, each with a single man at their entrance. Emma would guess those were supplies and arms, respectively.

She passed the leader's tent for now, sneaking around the two other larger tents. Their backs were unguarded, holes in the fence easy to slip through. She peeked inside both of them, slicing small rents in the canvas. The dim light inside showed crates, shelves, and tables. A quick glance confirmed them as scavenged supplies and some shelf stable goods, but she didn't need to do an inventory. She only needed to destroy them.

She sneaked away, crawling through the brush, making as little noise as possible, holding her breath close. The horse and Billy waited for her, just where she left them. She rooted around in her pack and found the packages she had taken from Trevor. He had offered them, free of charge, and it wasn't like Emma to look a gift horse in the mouth.

Emma moved fast now, confidently. Her joints ached, but she ignored the pain. There would be time for it later, when she was resting by the fire. Now she had to move, and she crept back through the brush, confirming the location of all the men. She saw it all now, saw it like clockwork, how they would move in reaction to every action.

Back into the supply tents, first one, then the other. She placed the first firebomb, and then the second, lighting each. They were short fuses, only a minute, but that was plenty of time. She pulled the lighter from her pouch, from the old world, heavy metal. It had cost her dearly to acquire it, but it had paid off a hundred times since then, and the fuses burnt down and she crept back, right in the position.

BOOM.

A few empty moments.

BOOM.

The two bombs went off, explosions of fire and destruction as flames enveloped the tents. Men shouted, running to them to put out the fire. They all knew where their food came from, and they rushed to the river, filling buckets, but the fuel in those bombs burned hot, and it would take a lot of water to put them out. It all happened quickly, but Emma was already moving toward the leader's tent, her knife in her offhand, her other hand ready to draw at a moment's notice. Firing her gun was a losing proposition, and she wouldn't do it unless she absolutely had to.

The guards had run off, and there were no other eyes on it. No one else had left the tent. They were still inside. Emma peeked in, ready to attack. She saw the leader, dressed in a long duster, bent over something, a box maybe? Emma didn't know, but she wasn't going to give him a fair fight. He was bigger than her, and from what Trevor had said, a hard man. She would do what was necessary.

She moved in behind him, without a sound. Emma grabbed his short red hair in one hand, yanked his head back, and slid the blade of the dagger across his neck, hard, deep enough to cut through his windpipe. The man choked, trying to breathe but only finding blood as it fountained out of his throat. Emma pulled him back to the ground, and his eyes stared wide at her, unbelieving, this being the last thing he expected. He stared at her, grabbing at her with soft, weakening, grasping hands. Red pointed, pointed at the crate he was overlooking. He mouthed a word to her

Please

And then he died, his eyes staring blankly. She shut them.

Emma should have left. Her mission was over. But her curiosity got the better of her, and she looked to the box that the man had been inspecting.

She stood, and saw now that it wasn't a box at all, or a crate.

It was a crib.

Inside laid an infant, softly sleeping.

<h1 style="text-align:center">6</h1>

"What's in the bundle, Emma?"

Billy's voice drifted up to Emma as she rode. She needed to make distance before she could camp down for the night. The explosions would draw attention for miles. She needed to make distance.

Emma ignored Billy.

"Emma, what did you do?" he asked. "You didn't—"

"I couldn't leave him," said Emma. "God knows what they'd do with him without his dad there. I had to do something."

Emma held the baby tight to her body. She had swaddled him, and then tied him tight to her chest, just like she had—

"You coulda just not killed his dad," said Billy. "Woulda made your choice easy."

"There aren't any easy choices out here," said Emma, practically shouting. "You know that, good as anyone. I—"

"You didn't know," said Billy. "Guess *you're* allowed to use that as an excuse."

Emma's heart burned cold, and she said nothing back to Billy. She didn't know what she'd do with the baby, but she couldn't leave him. Trevor had said the group would fall apart without their leader, and without him there, would they just leave his kid? She knew many a merc who would abandon a baby. Another mouth to feed when they couldn't feed their own. She had to take him. It was her responsibility now.

But what are you going to do with him, Emma? Are you going to ride out to the Wastelands with a baby? *In good conscience?*

"I can leave him with Trevor," said Emma. "He can raise him. Trevor's raised a boy before. He has the power."

She spoke aloud without realizing it, but Billy didn't answer. They rode in the dark, only the light from a slim moon guiding them. There was a risk of hurting the horse, but she rode until they were miles away, and then took the horse off into the brush, away from the road. As the horse bumped up and down on the uneven ground, the baby woke up and cried.

Emma rocked it softly as they rode, and then stopped the horse when they were a good distance from the path, dismounting, softly whispering to the baby as she rocked it. It would be hungry. It was old enough to eat food, at least. She grabbed her bedroll from the horse and let it graze. She couldn't build a fire, not after her attack.

The child wailed.

"Shh shh shh," said Emma. She grabbed her lone apple and peeled it deftly, her hand moving quickly, and took a big bite, chewing, chewing, chewing, until the bite was mush in her mouth, and she spat it out into her hand, grabbing her spoon, and feeding it to the child.

"Here you go," she said. "I'm sorry, it's all I have." The infant fed, consuming the apple mush. Emma continued until the apple was half gone and the baby ate no more. It stopped crying. It would need the bathroom soon. Emma would clean him when it was time. She propped her roll against a tree and sat back, softly rocking the boy. She sang, the only lullaby she knew. Emma sang quietly, whispering the tune to the child's ears, and soon he slept.

Emma sang, and tears slipped down her cheeks until exhaustion took her.

*

Emma returned to the Mongers by the middle of the next day. She slept little, and was riding by the time there was enough light to see by. She changed the baby's wrap after it went in the night. It was hungry again, and she fed it the other half of the apple she had.

She went into the Mongers camp as soon as they opened the gate, not waiting for an escort, riding straight back to Trevor's office. He sat outside, smoking. A half-dozen Mongers loitered around them. She dismounted.

"Did you not tell me, or did you not know?" she asked, marching up to him, standing over him. He stared up at her, raising an eyebrow.

"What are you talking about, Emma?" he asked.

Emma peeled back a layer of cloth to show the baby swaddled to her chest. It was awake, but quiet.

"You asked me to kill a man with a newborn," said Emma. "How could you—"

"I didn't know, Emma," said Trevor. "But it doesn't change anything. I assume the deed is done?"

"Yes, it's done," said Emma. "Their supplies are gone, and their leader is dead, and now this baby has no father."

"Why did you take it?" asked Trevor. "Surely one of the Gloves would have taken it—"

"Why would they?" asked Emma. "You yourself said they showed no loyalty to the man. Why would they raise his son in his stead?"

"I don't know," said Trevor. "But it's one child. What does it matter?"

"What does it matter?" asked Emma. She exhaled. "I'm leaving him with you."

"Excuse me?" asked Trevor. "That is not a part of our deal."

"It is now," said Emma. "You wanted the man dead, his child is now your responsibility. It is only right."

"I'm not in the business of right, Emma," said Trevor. "I have enough mouths to feed—"

"Then what's one more?"

"I am not a nursemaid, to watch over children," said Trevor, standing up. "You shouldn't have taken him if you were not prepared to take care of him yourself. You couldn't even keep your own kid alive and you're already saving another—"

Emma pulled her revolver then, the barrel between Trevor's eyes. "If you say anything more, make it a prayer."

The Mongers drew their own weapons, aiming at her.

Trevor didn't flinch. "Did you think I didn't know, Emma? It only makes sense, of course. What else could push Emma and James Burns to The City?"

"You have no idea what you're talking about," said Emma.

"Get that weapon out of my face, Emma. We'll gun you down, baby or not."

Emma held the pistol still.

"Sir, sir!" shouted a Monger, as he ran up into the stand-off.

"We're kind of busy here, Jones," said Trevor, not taking his eyes off Emma.

"The City is coming," said Jones, his chest heaving, sweat dripping off his forehead.

"What?"

"The City," said Jones, collecting himself. "Troops are on their way."

"You know about this, Emma? You lead them here?"

"Why the fuck would I do that? You think this is a ruse for you? Go fuck yourself."

"How many, Jones?" asked Trevor.

"Over a hundred," said Jones. "They'll be here in minutes."

"Emma, please drop your gun, so we can defend our stronghold," said Trevor.

"Only if you take the child," said Emma. "I can't keep him, I can't—"

"Oh, for fucks sake," said Trevor, walking away from her pistol. "Man the walls, we can keep them out, no matter how many there are—"

"Sir, they have war machines," said Jones, his eyes wide.

"What do you mean?" asked Trevor. "Out here? That's impossible."

"No, sir, our scouts reported multiple machines, rolling this—"

There was a distant BOOM, and then the wall exploded, fire and rock flying into the air. Emma ducked instinctively, shielding the baby.

"No," said Trevor. "Not yet. We had time, we had time, they wouldn't push this far yet—"

Another BOOM, and the wall shattered again, and then an explosion inside the fort, and Emma was running, her arms cradling the infant. Her horse was there, and it bucked and whinnied as explosions rocked around them, but Emma grabbed its reins and hopped up in a quick motion, even as it moved in fear. She pulled it tight and set it at a gallop, even as the whistling shells landed behind her. She didn't look back.

Her ears rang as the outbuildings exploded around her, showering the area with shrapnel and stone. The City was here, to take back what once belonged to them, so long ago. Trevor should have known better. The City wouldn't stand for one organized gang, not in a stronghold like this. They would cut off the snake's head before it could grow too large.

Emma galloped hard through the interior of the fort. She pushed the horse hard to the gates, one of them hanging off its side, an explosion destroying the arch it once framed.

She had seen the war machines in The City, once. When she and James had first arrived, and surrendered their arms and signed their paperwork. The massive things had sat outside, weighing 60 tons and towering over both of them. She had heard of them, of course, of the great machines of the old world, dug up, cleaned, and repaired using the knowledge unearthed and passed down. It was the backbone of the strength of The City. She could scarcely believe them.

But she had never seen them move. Or fire.

Trevor had fought for years to get to the size where he could take that stronghold. Where he could drive out whoever held it, repair it, and recruit enough men to hold it. And then maintain enough supplies to feed that size force.

But his dozens of men didn't matter, because The City could do that, and take it from him in moments.

Not even take it. They didn't want to hold the fort. They only wanted to destroy it, and crush The Mongers.

Emma rode out of the gate of the stronghold and looked behind her, one time, as she turned the horse west. Smoke rose in the distance, but she didn't see the troops. Not yet. She hoped the fort was all they wanted.

She rode, pushing the horse as hard as it could, her ears still ringing. The sound of the baby crying made her realize they had been riding for a long while, the noise of the battle gone behind them. She stopped, pulling the horse to the side of the road, dismounting. She leaned against the neck of the animal, and closed her eyes. Emma caught her breath.

She fed and changed the baby again. Emma was running out of clean cloth. She would need to stop by the river at some point.

"I'll find a home for you," said Emma. "I promise."

"Out here?" asked Billy.

Emma didn't answer him.

"Turn around, Emma," said Billy. "The City will still take you. Give that child a safe place to grow up."

Emma mounted her horse again and rode west.

7

Emma was exhausted, running on little sleep, frazzled by the attack on the fort by The City, but she rode until dark, west, west, toward the Wastelands.

She made camp when it was too dark to ride, fearful of breaking her horse and being stranded in The Frontier, not even to The Scraps before her journey would end.

The baby cried, and Emma fed it. She had little fruit left in her packs, precious fruit, even more precious out here. But she fed it all to the baby and changed his clothes one more time. She would have to stop at the river tomorrow, and wash if this would continue. The food, the change, and the fire lulled the baby back to sleep. Emma gently rocked it and then tied it to her chest once again—

Just like little Thomas—

Emma cut off the thought, and stared into the fire. Her horse grazed nearby, eating at the grass.

"What's your plan with that kid?" asked Billy.

"What do you care?" asked Emma.

"I'm not a monster, Emma," said Billy. "I'm the same guy you worked with for years—"

"You're not the same, Billy," said Emma. "The Billy I knew would have never—"

"I'm the one who's dead, Emma," said Billy. "Not you—"

"I did what I had to do."

"Like with the Gloves leader?" asked Billy. "You killed him for nothing. Made this boy an orphan for *nothing*."

"I did what I had to do," said Emma. "Trevor wanted him dead, so I made him dead. Like I've killed many others. That is what life is out here, Billy. Out here, everyone plays the same game, and they know it. You don't lead a gang without knowing you could die at any moment. That man made the choice to raise a child out here. Would it change anything if someone else had killed him? If some Monger hunted him down and left the kid to starve? At least I took the child. I'll find a home for him. Do you remember your parents?"

"No."

"And neither do I," said Emma. "I'll find him a home before we head into The Scraps. There'll be a town up ahead. Every town has a barren mother looking for a child to raise. He'll be safer there than he would be in some encampment. Especially with The City moving in."

"They're following us."

"Don't be stupid," said Emma. "The City isn't going to send war machines and a hundred troops over a heretic. Trevor thought he could hold that fort, and build up The

Mongers into something formidable. Maybe even something that could hold off The City for a while longer. And The City caught wind of it. Maybe even saw it, with their eyes in the sky."

"I thought those were a myth."

"I saw one flying over The City," said Emma. "Glinted in the sun. They've got whole teams salvaging old world tech and making it new again. They weren't going to let some pissant gang hold a stronghold, not when they could blow it up with a nice display of force."

"Do you think Trevor made it?"

"I don't know," said Emma. "Probably not."

The fire popped and crackled, and the warmth felt good as the night chill settled in.

"You don't have to do this, Emma," said Billy.

"Don't start."

"Or what? What else can you take from me?" asked Billy. "You can't shut me up. You'll just have to listen."

Emma stared into the fire. The warmth of the child settled into her chest and her breath was heavy and she slept.

"Moooooom," said a voice, intruding on her sleep. Her mind was in the place between awake and sleep, struggling between both, and then she felt the impact of a body slam next to her on the mattress.

"Mooom," said the voice again. "You said we could have pancakes this morning."

Emma opened her eyes to see Thomas, blond hair that was already turning brown, freckles spotting his nose. His freckles were the only thing he carried from her, his freckles and maybe the corner of his eyes when he smiled, which he was doing now. He laid next to her in bed. James had gotten up early to do chores, but she had slept in.

Sleeping in wasn't a concept she understood, not for the longest time. Her body woke her up right before dawn, every day, had because it kept her alive. Had because getting up before everyone else made her ready for whatever was coming. She knew men who could sleep through anything, sleep on a rock with dirt for a blanket and never wake up unless prodded. Not her, though.

But she had never imagined this life, and now James would leave her to sleep in when she said, and today was one of those days, where the sun had risen hours ago, and the bed was warm and soft and the deep parts of her mind tried to keep her there. But she didn't mind being woken by Thomas, her son, the kindest and softest boy she'd ever known. If you had shown her this child years ago, she would have never guessed it was her boy. She would never raise a child to be soft. To be kind. It was irresponsible to do so, especially in this world. The child would die as soon as it left your sight. Some thief or bandit or monster would take them and use them for whatever they needed.

But she had never envisioned this life, had never seen this as a possibility. Their own land and home. Safe from bandits and intruders. A bed to call their own, even. And she saw Thomas for what he was.

A miracle.

"Morning, Thomas," said Emma, wiping the sleep from her eyes.

"Pancakes?" he asked, smiling.

"Yes, dear, pancakes," said Emma. "Just give me a few minutes to wake up."

"Dad made coffee and left some for you," said Thomas.

"He told me to tell you."

"I'll take him up on that," said Emma. "Go get the ingredients ready. I'll be out in a minute, okay?"

"Okay!" yelled Thomas as he jumped out of the bed and sprinted down the hallway into the kitchen. She heard him rattling around. She'd gotten the recipe from a neighbor. Another concept that was hard to understand. People who lived nearby that she could trust not to steal or kill while she slept.

She forced herself out of bed. Her back popped as she stood up, and then her knees followed, two pistol shots as she walked to the bathroom, did her business, and then changed into house clothes.

Thomas had the flour, eggs, milk, and butter already out on the counter by the time she came out. He held the recipe in his hands, studying it like a monk would study a massive Bible, trying to glean important, deep knowledge from it.

"Where's the sugar?" asked Emma.

"I can't reach it," said Thomas. Emma smiled and grabbed it, high from the cabinet.

The flour and sugar was bought, but the eggs, milk, and butter were all made by them. The City had given them the land, and the stock, and that was all they needed.

"Can't make pancakes by reading," said Emma. "Only by doing."

"I can do it," said Thomas. Emma checked the fire in the stove, and it still burned, and she threw on a log.

"I'll let you take charge," said Emma. "We can mix up the batter while the stove heats up."

Thomas grabbed the measuring cups from the cabinet, and a massive bowl, almost bigger than him, and a big wooden spoon. He carefully measured the flour. He cracked the eggs, poured in the milk, and then dropped in the butter, softened.

"Now, stir," said Emma. "But don't stir too much. Don't want tough pancakes."

"I knooow," he said, grabbing the wooden spoon in two hands and stirring, breaking up the eggs, and watching as the flour absorbed everything else.

"You think that's enough?" asked Emma, testing him.

"No, not yet," said Thomas. "One more minute." She didn't stop him, letting him go. Letting him learn.

"There," he said. "It's ready. Is the stove hot enough?"

She waved a hand over the pan on the stove, and it felt right.

"I think so," she said. She grabbed the bowl and moved it over closer to the stove.

"Can I pour them, Mom?" he asked, his eyes wide.

"Not yet, Thomas," said Emma. "You can supervise. But you're not ready for the stove. It's dangerous."

"I can handle it," said Thomas. "I'll be careful."

"It has nothing to do with careful," said Emma. "The pan is heavy, and you're not strong enough yet."

Thomas pouted. "Fine."

"Go get your dad," she said. "By the time you find him, breakfast will be ready."

Thomas nodded, happy to have something to do, and ran out the back door, out onto their farm. James was probably tending the cattle, and it'd take Thomas about ten minutes to get him. Enough time for Emma to make pancakes.

The house was silent, except for gentle whistling as she poured the batter into the pan. But she wasn't really listening. She cooked, her attention only on the food, flipping them when necessary, and stacking them up on a plate.

She wasn't listening for approaching hooves, or distant gunfire. She wasn't thinking about their next score.

She just made pancakes.

The door opened, and she looked to see James' smiling face, as he wiped his face with a cloth. Thomas followed in right behind him.

"I was told there were pancakes?" he asked. James was tall, and lean, with thick black hair cut short on his head. Streaks of gray ran at his temples, but they only made him more attractive to her. His sleeves were rolled halfway up his forearms, and he washed his hands under the faucet.

"A little birdie told you, huh?" asked Emma.

"It wasn't a birdie. It was me," said Thomas, smiling, walking up close to inspect the pancakes.

"How do they look?" asked Emma.

"They look great," said Thomas. He slowly reached out to sneak a bite.

"Wait two minutes and you can eat with us," said Emma. "Jeez, the food isn't going to fly away."

"Come sit down, son," said James. James grabbed the butter and put it on the table, and grabbed them each a plate. Emma flipped the last pancake onto the stack, and then carried it over. She slid a pair of pancakes to each of her and James and then gave Thomas one.

"I want two," said Thomas.

"Finish one, and then you can have another," said Emma. James was already eating, after slathering both of his pancakes with butter.

"Fantastic, honey," said James. "Your finest work yet."

"It was all Thomas," said Emma.

CLICK

"Did you hear that?" asked Emma, looking around. That didn't belong, that was a sound from another time, another place, there was nothing here but family and pancakes, and she looked to Thomas and blood ran from his mouth—

CLICK.

Emma opened her eyes.

CLICK.

The fire filled her vision. It was still dark, the baby still clutched tight to her chest.

CLICK.

She looked to the source of the sound, not the fire, but past it, to the other side. A man sat there, his eyes glowing in the dark. She saw his eyes, and then the heavy hand cannon that was aimed at her. The man cocked it CLICK and then uncocked it CLICK. Her eyes flicked to the gun, and then to his clothes. A City Ranger. He cocked the gun again CLICK.

"Sorry," he said. "Bad habit."

CLICK.

CLICK.

8

"I know what you're thinking," said the ranger. "Don't. I don't want to kill you."

Emma stared across the fire at him. His eyes glowed, his brown skin contrasted against the green of his uniform. He wore a cavalry hat, emblazoned with the icon of The City. Her gaze flitted to his pistol. It stayed leveled at her.

"If you're a ranger, you're a good shot," said Emma.

"I am," said the ranger. His voice was deep and velvet, rumbling in his chest.

"How did I not hear you?" asked Emma.

"Everyone knows you, Mrs. Burns," said the ranger. "You're a legend. Sharpest eyes and ears in the Kingdom. Good with your gun, but it's not the gun that kills anyone. It's your eyes. Your ears. That's why they put me on you. No one in the whole Corps as quiet as me."

"Can I get your name?"

"Holloway," he said. He tipped his cap.

"I would say it was a pleasure, but I won't lie to a ranger. How did you find me?"

"Trevor," said Holloway.

"That son of a bitch," said Emma.

"They leaned on him and he told us where you were headed," said Holloway. "Not that it was much of a mystery. Don't hold it against him. I would have found you, anyway. Who's kid is that?"

"Leader of the Gloves."

"Any reason you took him?"

"Yeah, his dad is dead," said Emma. "The gang would have left him to starve. I took him so he wouldn't die."

Holloway raised an eyebrow. "You sure that's the reason you took him?"

"Yeah," said Emma. "I'm sure."

"Fair enough," said Holloway. "Will you come back peacefully? Or will I have to restrain you?"

Emma stared at him. "You don't have to take me back. I'm not hurting anyone."

"That corpse tied to your horse might say something different," said Holloway. "Mr. Brunner was alive until you shot him."

"He deserved it," said Emma. "For what he did."

"That may be so," said Holloway. "But it's not up to you to decide."

"Then who? You?"

"No," said Holloway. "The City. The courts. They would mete the justice necessary. If that ended up being execution, so be it. But we can't allow for vigilante justice. And we certainly can't allow heresy. It's dangerous. We've finally got to a point where we're stamping it out."

"It's not your business."

"You lived in The City, Mrs. Burns," said Holloway. "You should know better than that. It is absolutely our business. We can't have people dealing out justice, especially within City limits. Not up to you."

A tear trickled down Emma's cheek. "He killed my son."

"And you have my condolences," said Holloway. "But it doesn't change the fact that we must go back to The City. His body will be burnt in line with City protocol. His crime will most likely ease the punishment of your vigilantism."

"He deserves worse," said Emma. "He shouldn't get a cremation, in some City mortuary. He doesn't deserve Heaven."

Holloway narrowed his eyes, studying her, trying to read her. Emma stared back, unflinching.

"Do you really believe that?" asked Holloway.

"Believe what?"

"Believe in that superstition?" said Holloway. His voice was measured, but Emma still heard the condescension there. "Believe that if you bury him out there in The Wastelands, that'll he rot in hell? That the location of his physical body affects the location of his immortal soul?"

Emma stared at him, feeling an anger rise in her.

"Why would I be doing this if I didn't believe?"

"There could be many reasons," said Holloway. "I've encountered them in all manners of ways as I've gone about my job. Rooting out heresy is customary, and I've largely found that people don't believe what they believe."

"What the hell does that mean?"

"It means that their beliefs reflect what they want from the world. Their belief comes from desire, not from observable evidence. You want justice in your world, and so that shapes your beliefs. You believe because you fear your desired world doesn't exist."

"Are you—are you calling me a coward?"

"No," said Holloway. "Because that might not be the truth, for you. I don't think it is, honestly. I think the alternative is much more likely."

"And what's that?"

"That you don't believe at all."

"Is that right?"

"Yes," said Holloway. His gun stayed level, still pointed right at her. It was a heavy pistol, but Holloway's arm didn't tremble. He was as sturdy as a rock. "I think this man committed a great sin against you, and you searched for the greatest retribution possible. You have already killed him, but that didn't ease your vengeance. What else is left?"

The fire cracked and popped between them.

"What do *you* believe, Ranger Holloway?" asked Emma. "You seem to have a lot of thoughts about it."

Holloway smiled. "I believe in the future, Mrs. Burns. I believe in The City. I believe if we continue on our current path, the world will be a better place."

Emma stared at him. "You can believe all of that if you want. But don't tell me what I believe," said Emma. "Ranger or not."

"Fair enough," said Holloway. "It doesn't change the fact that I cannot allow you to take the body any farther. We will return to The City. All of us."

"I'm not going back until Billy is buried where he belongs."

"This is not a negotiation," said Holloway. "It is simply the way things will be."

"Your ranger talk isn't going to work on me," said Emma. "I'm not some young moron, grown to be afraid of you. You're just a man in a uniform. I've killed lots of them in my time."

Holloway's face grew grim.

"I *will* kill you, Mrs. Burns. I don't want to return you to your husband a corpse, but I have my duty, and I will abide it," said Holloway.

"You said you're a good shot," said Emma. "Are you?"

Holloway exhaled through his nose. "Yes." The gun was still leveled at her.

"Aren't you concerned about hitting the baby? Isn't it Ranger doctrine to not hurt the innocent?"

"It is," said Holloway. "But I won't hit the child."

"Are you sure?" asked Emma. "What if I move unexpectedly? One foot up or down, and your bullet kills him, and not me. I fire, and you die."

"I don't think you would sacrifice a child's life you went so far to save," said Holloway. "Seems unlikely. Please surrender."

The silence hung between them, and the fire crackled.

A voice spoke to her from the darkness.

"Do you think I'm a good person, Holloway?" asked Emma.

"I don't see what—"

"Answer the question," said Emma. "If you want me to come along peacefully, answer the question."

Holloway looked into her eyes.

"No, Mrs. Burns," he said. "You're not a good person. A good person, living the way you've lived, would have died long ago. They would have lost their nerve. They would have taken a life, and felt such horror and remorse that they would have given up, and been killed by someone else who was harder. Someone like you."

Emma nodded. "Are you any better?"

"Oh, no," said Holloway. "Of course not. I carry no illusion about my role. I am a bridge, Mrs. Burns. And after I help lead us to the next step on our journey, I will be burned." He paused. "Did I answer your question?"

"Yes," said Emma. "I'm going to stand up, okay?"

"Okay," said Holloway. "Move slowly. Walk toward me, and I will take your pistol from you." Holloway stood, waiting for her.

Emma stood slowly, letting Holloway see her actions. The baby still slept against her chest. She rose with practiced motion, watching Holloway's eyes. He watched her hands, and then for a moment his eyes flicked to her pistol, and she moved, a tiny, swift movement.

If Holloway noticed, he said nothing, did nothing differently. He reached down, and grabbed her pistol from her with his free hand, his gun pointed at her, the heavy cannon leveled at her, his arm still not trembling.

It wouldn't take long, and Emma watched and waited. Holloway held her pistol now.

"I'll rope our horses together," said Holloway. "And you'll ride in front of me. Understood?"

Emma nodded. She would have to move quickly, and hope Holloway would be caught off guard. She paused, waiting by the fire, delaying as long as she could.

"Come on," he said.

"Just trying to keep the child warm," she said. "Do you have kids, Ranger?" She stared at him as she asked, even if she already knew the answer.

"No, it's forbidden—"

And then the bullet she dropped in the flames fired, one sudden BANG and she reacted immediately. The noise surprised Holloway, only a moment, but enough time for Emma. She stepped inside his grasp so he couldn't fire and brought the heel of her boot down as hard as she could on his shin, the side of her heel scraping down skin and bone and then she brought her knee up into his groin. Both strikes hit hard, but she wasn't done. They were only to buy her time, another moment to strike.

She reared back and headbutted him on the bridge of his nose and was rewarded with a CRACK as his nose broke and he fell. As he dropped she reached and took her gun back from his hand, and kicked the wrist that held his own pistol. Another SNAP as his wrist fractured.

He laid now, dazed. She pointed her gun at him.

"You shouldn't have woken me up," said Emma. "You damn rangers. Think you're so smart."

"I was trying to help you," said Holloway, groaning on the ground.

"You did help me, Ranger," said Emma. "And you still will."

"Oh, go fuck yourself," said Holloway. "You broke my fucking wrist. I can't defend myself."

"All you have to do is make it back to your troops," said Emma. "It's a few hours ride. You'll be fine."

"They'll send someone else—"

"I'm sure they will," said Emma. "But they won't find me. Not again."

Holloway seethed on the ground, clutching his broken wrist.

"Don't get up," said Emma. "I don't want to kill you."

"You bitch," said Holloway. "What are you going to do? Take that baby into The Wasteland?"

"No," said Emma. "I'm going to make a bet."

"What?" asked Holloway, his face full of confusion.

"I'm going to bet that you're a liar," said Emma.

"I—"

"I'm going to bet that you *are* a good man," said Emma. "A good person, in all the ways that I am not." She unwrapped the child from her chest, and it woke, and murmured dissent. She held him out to Holloway. "Take him."

"What? No."

"You will take him, or you will die," said Emma, holding the gun to his head. "It's a simple bet. I bet you are a good man, and I bet you value this child's life, and I bet you value your own."

Holloway stared at her, and then took the swaddled child from her with his good arm, cradling the child against him.

"Take him back to The City," said Emma. "Give him a good life." Emma grabbed her bedroll and threw it on her horse, and then rode away in the dark.

9

"What did I say? What did I say?" asked Billy as they rode through the dark. It wasn't long before the sun rose behind the horizon, and her worries about crippling her horse eased as the dull light grew bright enough to see by.

"Credit where it's due," said Emma, an easy idiom that they had used all the time back in the day. Even to the dumbest dullard, if they did something right, credit where it's due.

Even when the man had killed your son.

"Rangers can't think their way around problems," said Billy. "They always think in straight lines. A little bullet in the campfire trick. Can't believe he fell for it."

Billy had given her the idea right when she needed it.

"Why did you help me?" asked Emma.

You know why, Emma. Because—

"Because he's a damnable ranger, Emma. I don't care what you did, there's no way in Hell I'm helping a ranger, if I can help it. My only problem is that you left him alive."

"I had to. He'll be busy with the kid now, and we can go on our way."

"But he can still follow us—"

"I broke his wrist, Billy. If he still follows us, he's a damned fool, even more than we already thought. Plus, he'll make sure to take the baby back to The City."

"How do you know that?" asked Billy.

"Because he's a good man," said Emma.

"Funny, he said the exact opposite," said Billy. "Rambling on and on about ethics and morals and all that other bull-shit. Jesus Christ, if I wasn't already dead, I would have shot myself, just so I didn't have to hear it anymore."

"I've looked into the eyes of a lot of bad men, Billy. Holloway isn't one of them. Maybe he likes to tell himself that, because he's young and still thinks of the world in that way. But he's not a bad person. A bad man would have shot me in my sleep and left the child to die. There are rangers who've done much worse. But Holloway's not one of them. He'll take the boy back to The City, and report his failure. They'll send someone else, but they'll take a long time to catch up to us. And they won't follow us past The Scraps."

"You sure you're not just saying that because you left the kid with him?" asked Billy. Emma didn't answer. She had slept little the past few nights, but she rode on. Her encounter with the ranger had given her a burst of energy, her dream about Thomas and James mostly forgotten. They were nearing the end of The Frontier. The Scraps were next, but they needed supplies before they went out there. Supplies and all the intel she could manage.

They rode into Last Stop around noon, the sun high in the sky. The trees thinned as they went farther west, the ground becoming rockier and more barren. Less cover. Emma's ears and eyes didn't stop working, not out here, but she had less worry about ambushes. There weren't enough travelers to warrant bandits. Agatha was still out there, somewhere, but Emma would hear her coming a mile away.

Last Stop was just that, the last town within fifty miles that had any semblance of law and order. Not much of a town, with a handful of tiny row houses, plus a sheriff, a general store, and a tiny inn.

Emma tied her horse in front of the sheriff. He sat outside his office, an old man chewing tobacco, spitting wads of brown saliva into his spittoon. He eyed her and she nodded at him, tipping her hat. The sheriff tipped it back. She'd be back to talk to him, but there wasn't no safer place for her horse and Billy than right there in front of him. The packed dirt of the small road that ran through the town echoed beneath her feet as she went to the general store. A small man sat behind the counter, bent glasses crooked over his nose. He held a narrow book, the pages ragged and torn. He put it down as she entered.

"How can I help you?"

She looked around the store, various shelves filled with trinkets and sundries.

"What do you carry?" asked Emma.

"Whatever I can get my hands on," said the shopkeep. "What do you need?"

"Ammo. Rations," said Emma. "As much as you have."

"What kind of ammo?" he asked. Emma fished into a pouch at her hip and placed a shell on the counter.

"These."

He nodded and reached under the counter. "I've got one box," he said, bringing it out. The small box was worn and frayed, taken from somewhere in the Scraps, long ago, passing hands back and forth until it ended up here. He eyed the gun at her waist. "I don't want any funny business. Sheriff is just two lots over."

"I've got the gold to pay," said Emma. "Don't you worry. How much?"

"Ten."

"How many rations do you have?"

"Not much," he said. "Couple weeks worth. Good stock. From The Scraps. No rot or bugs."

"I'll take them all."

"All of it?" asked the shopkeep. "Is it just you?"

"Yeah, it's just me," she said. "All of it."

"That'll be another ten," he said. He grabbed a wooden box from behind the counter and placed it next to the shells. Emma peeked in, and the ration packs were sturdy, still sealed. "Anything else?"

"Do you have any rad pills?"

"Rad pills?" asked the shopkeep. "You going out to the Wastes?"

"Do you have them or not?"

"No," said the shopkeep. "Haven't seen any in a long time. I ask every trader that comes through, but if anyone has them, they're holding onto them. Maybe try your luck out in The Scraps."

"You trying to be clever with me?"

"No, ma'am," he said, holding his hands up, his palms out. "I heard word that there still might be sources out there for the pills. People sitting on 'em."

"Yeah, sure," said Emma. "Twenty gold, then?"

"Yes," he said. She reached into her pouch and pulled out the pieces, handing them over.

"Holy shit, City gold," he said, examining the metal. Emma left him to study his new money and threw the shells in the box with the rations, taking them back to her horse, and slowly loading them into the compartments that hung off her saddle. Two weeks of rations should be plenty. Plenty, as long as she kept it all.

The sheriff watched her as she unloaded and reloaded her supplies, taking the shells and sliding them into pouches on her belt. Unless she got into multiple firefights, she'd have enough ammo.

Her supplies stowed, she glanced at the sheriff, who hadn't moved since she'd rode into town.

"You have a moment to talk?" she asked.

"Naw, too dang busy," said the man. "You'll have to come back." He winked at her and then gestured to the seat next to him with his head. "Come on. Have a seat."

The sheriff was old, in his 60s, but hard to tell, with the effect of hard living on people. He wore khaki pants and a dark button-up shirt. The top half of the buttons hung undone. A revolver sat on his belt, holstered in a piece of beaten leather.

Emma seldom met people older than her, especially out here. No one lived into old age without a combination of guile, luck, and quick thinking. She sat down next to him, glad to be out of the sun for a moment.

"Are you Emma Burns?" he asked, his voice dark and low, but with a gentle lilt, all that time spent out here in this wild land not enough to erase it.

"Yeah, that's me," said Emma. "Heard of me?"

"You could say that," said the lawman. "How many other women of your age, with that gun, with a body on the back of their horse comes around?"

"We have trouble?"

"Oh, none at all," said the lawman. "I didn't get old by picking fights with just anybody who came through town."

"Can I have your name?"

"Cody Dean," he said. "Seems only fair. You can just call me Cody. Not like anybody ever made me Sheriff, anyway."

"I'm looking for information."

"'Bout what?"

"About what's ahead," said Emma. Cody gave her a sideways glance.

"I'll make you a deal," said Cody. "You tell me what's coming, and I'll tell you what's ahead of you. Sound good?"

"Sounds good to me," said Emma. "So?"

Cody laughed. "I guess I should go first, the gentleman I am. You ever been to The Scraps?"

"It's been a long, long time," said Emma.

"Well, it ain't gotten better, I'll tell you that," he said. "Scavvers, bandits, traders have ripped it up, and pulled out most anything that's worth more than nothing. Plus, the rads are leaking out into the land."

"That far?" asked Emma.

"Yep," said Cody. "Used to be that a body could live out in The Scraps, if they could find the things to live on, you know? But I keep hearing stories about cancer. About mutation. I don't know, but I wouldn't go out there."

"I ain't got no choice."

"There's always a choice," said Cody. "Just sometimes it ain't nothing but bad ones." He gestured toward the body. "You taking him out there?"

Emma paused. "Yeah."

"What'd he do?"

"He killed my son," said Emma. "Gunned him down."

Cody nodded. "That's where he belongs, then. But it'll be hell to get there. Even beyond The Scraps. You got any rad pills?"

"No," said Emma.

"Remnants are worse, too, from what I hear. But I only hear a little. No one goes out there anymore. Wouldn't venture even that far without the pills. Hear there's something stalking the old world."

"What is it?"

"I don't know," said Cody. "You wanted to know what I heard, that's what I've heard. All with a grain of salt. I barely leave this stoop."

Emma chuckled, a smile an alien sensation.

"Anything behind you I should know about?" asked Cody.

"Mongers and Gloves are both done," said Emma.

"Both of 'em?"

"Yeah," said Emma. "I finished the Gloves, and The City took the Mongers out. That ole fort, stronghold, whatever you want to call it. City blew it up. Marched their war machines out into the West."

"Damn," said Cody. "They keep pushing, don't they? I remember when they were a joke. I was a teenager when their forces took the city, back before it was *The City*, you know? We all thought it was stupid. Trying to enforce law on the lawless. And now—now there ain't much but them, huh?"

"They'll be out this far by this time next year, I reckon," said Emma. "They're pushing hard. Expanding."

"It was a matter of time," said Cody. "Doubt they'll put too much of a fuss over an old lawman."

"They'll give you something to do."

"I kinda like sitting here and pretending I'm important."

"They'll probably keep letting you do that," said Emma. "It's mostly my type they ain't fond of."

"It's the way of things."

"What is?"

"The City coming out, taking things over," said Cody. "Killing whatever kind of life we've built out here on our own. We've made due with the cards we were dealt, and they'll end it without a thought. But it was only a matter of time. Anything else I should know about?"

"You know an Agatha Brunner? Heard of her?"

"Can't say that I have."

"Big woman, well armed, riding with a dozen men. They're killers. Give them what they want, if they come through."

"What will they want?"

"They'll want to know where I am."

"What do I tell 'em?"

"You tell them the truth. Tell them I'm sending Billy to Hell."

10

"Put your fucking hands up!" yelled James as they burst into the bank.

It was a plain wooden building, in a town called Rockwall, that had built up over the last couple years. They had suspected there was City influence there, that they had sent the mayor to drum up support for The City as it moved west.

It was a reason to hit it, but it wasn't *the* reason, not really. The reason was its gold. It had a lot of it, at least that's what they heard.

There were only a few people inside, a single teller, a manager, a couple customers. Emma's crew numbered eight. Emma, James, Agatha, Billy, Lizzie, Tom, Elijah, and Steven. All of them well armed, and the four in the bank all raised their arms into the sky.

But there was one more inside, and he didn't raise his arms.

The guard, tucked back into an alcove beside the door, emerged with his pistol drawn. He fired once, BANG.

Emma turned and shot him down, her shot BANG going off just after he fired.

He fell with a thump, her shot hitting him in the eye, killing him before he hit the ground. His gun fell beside him. The rest of the employees watched in shocked silence.

"Fuck!" yelled Billy, clutching his head. Agatha looked at him.

"Billy," she said, her voice hushed.

"I'm fine, I think," he said. He pulled his hand away. The bullet had grazed his temple. An inch to the left and he'd have been a goner.

James looked at the employees and marched to the manager, jumping over the counter, holding his pistol to his head.

"Key to the safe," said James, his normally soft voice a bark.

The manager only stared, his eyes full of fear. None of the other employees had moved, and the rest of the crew moved into the bank, with Lizzie and Steven watching the door.

"Don't make me repeat myself," said James.

The manager stared. His lips parted. "N-no," he said, his voice trembling.

"Excuse me?" asked James. "If you'd like your brains to stay inside your head, I'd ask you to reconsider."

"I can't," he said, slightly more firm. "He'll—"

"Oh, fuck this," said Agatha, who grabbed the teller around her neck, and marched her to the manager. "What's your name, girlie?"

"Sally," she said meekly.

"Give us the key to the safe, or Sally doesn't see tomorrow," said Agatha.

"You don't understand, I can't—"

Agatha smashed the butt of her revolver into Sally's face and her nose broke with a CRACK. She screamed in pain.

"The key," said Agatha. "Give it to us."

The manager stared at Agatha, who loomed over him. Sally was barely half her size. He said nothing, and Agatha hit her again. And then again, and again. Sally's face was covered in blood, streaming down over her eyes, mixing with tears.

"Agatha," said Emma, her voice curt. Agatha stopped.

"Give us the key," said James. "It's not your gold."

"The mayor—"

"The mayor will what?" asked James.

"The mayor'll fire me if I give it up—"

"I will *fire* this gun into Sally's pretty little face if you don't give us that key," said Agatha. "I'm done with this shit—"

"Please, Mr. Mortimer," said Sally, sobbing through blood.

"Agatha—" started Emma.

"No," she said. "5, 4, 3." She cocked the hammer on her big pistol, the barrel pointed at Sally's face. "2, 1—"

"Wait, wait, I have it, I have it!" yelled the manager, James' gun still aimed at him. He took off his shoe, and reached inside, and held out a strangely shaped key.

"Please, let her go," said the manager. Agatha stared at him, and dropped Sally to the floor, where she cried through her broken face.

James grabbed the key.

"The floor," said James, gesturing to the manager. He slid down, his eyes hollow. "Empty it." James handed the key off as they headed to the large safe.

*

They had settled into camp, miles away from town. They weren't invisible, but with how many armed people they had, only fools would attack them.

Even with the amount of gold they had stolen. It was a big haul, with most minted in a new form, unrecognizable to Emma.

"It's City gold," said James. "Has to be."

"City doesn't have gold," said Lizzie.

"Well, they don't have this gold," said Billy, smiling, sitting next to Agatha. She laughed. Her arm was over his shoulder, pulling him in close. They sat around the fire, at varying distances.

"The City is minting new gold," said Emma. "Or at least melting down what they've found."

"Spends just the same," said Agatha, her voice low.

"I don't like it," said James. "It's dangerous."

"Agatha's right, we can spend it all the same. Don't matter what shape it's in," said Lizzie.

"It does matter," said Emma.

"Who cares?" asked Billy. "We got it now."

"They care," said James. "The City cares. They're minting money. That's a big operation."

"They're just showing off," said Agatha, eyeing him.

"I don't think so," said Emma.

"They don't do anything without a reason," said James. "They're not showing off. They're spreading the word. And by spending this gold, that's exactly what we'll be doing. Everywhere this gold goes, The City goes. What's more powerful than gold?"

"A bullet," piped in Agatha. Billy laughed.

James ignored her. He held up a piece of the new gold. "Everywhere this goes, The City gets stronger." Emma watched everyone's eyes. She and James had discussed it in whispers, but she didn't think the group would go along. She told James as such. But he said they needed to hold their ground on it.

"What are you saying?" asked Agatha. Emma eyed her. She hadn't said it outright, but they both knew she was the key in any dissent.

"That we can't spend City gold," said James, finally, looking over the crew.

"The hell you say," said Elijah. He sat back, whittling, but now focused on James.

"We spent weeks plotting that hit," said Lizzie. "And now we don't spend half the loot?"

"If we don't spend it, what the fuck are we going to do with it?" asked Billy.

Agatha said nothing, only stared at James, and then flicked her eyes to Emma. Emma held her stare. Agatha narrowed her eyes, and looked back to James.

"I earned my share of the gold," said Agatha. "And you are not keeping it from me." Agatha's voice cut through the chatter, and everyone went silent. Emma let her hand linger near her revolver.

"You can have it if you want, Agatha," said James. "Your

share. But any more City gold we find, I plan on burying."

"What the fuck nonsense is this?" asked Agatha. No one else spoke, all watching her. Emma didn't know who believed what. Billy would back Agatha, most likely, but she didn't know about the rest.

"The City is spreading," said James. "They'll put an end to whatever life we have. It's their way or the highway."

"They can only spread so far, so fast," said Agatha. "Still plenty of territory for us."

"You say that now," said Emma. Agatha's eyes flicked to her.

"And I'll say it in ten years," said Agatha. "We'll all be dead by the time The City moves out here, and it's not on us to worry about spending their damned gold or not—"

"It's our land, Agatha, it's our choices that shape it—"

"Do-gooding bullshit," said Agatha. "I was the one who had to get that damned key from that fuckwit, I should decide who and how we spend it—"

"You smashed in a poor girl's face," said Emma. "God knows if she'll even heal right."

Agatha just stared at Emma and then started laughing. She laughed hard, staring the whole time, and then Billy laughed with her. Emma fixed her eyes on him, and he stopped.

Agatha stood up.

"What do you think we are, Emma?" asked Agatha, smiling. "Do you think we're Robin Hood? We rob and kill for a living."

"We do what is necessary," said Emma. "What we have to live—"

"Bullshit," said Agatha. "We are wolves, Emma. We are

killers. What the hell does it matter if we break some girl's face, as long as we get what we're after? What the hell does it matter if we spend City gold?"

"It ain't right, Agatha," said Emma. "There's a right way of doing things—"

"Oh, fuck off," said Agatha. Everyone else watched them now. The two strongest wills in the group, squaring off.

"You watch your—"

"I'll watch nothing," said Agatha. "I shoulder more than my fair share here, and I'll speak my mind. It needs to be said, and if it has to be me, so be it." She spit into the fire. "There isn't a kind way to do what we do. If you think that, you're sorely mistaken. If you think there's a difference between you and me, there ain't." She paused. "Pardon, there's one. The difference being that I know I'm a killer."

Agatha held Emma's stare for a second longer, and then marched away, back to her tent. Billy looked into Emma's cold eyes and then followed.

11

Emma woke early that morning in Last Stop, her mind awash in memories. She didn't try to reclaim sleep, and instead packed up and left.

They rode into The Scraps.

The change wasn't sudden, and there were no signposts that would tell you had left The Frontier behind, but Emma's eyes and ears could see and hear the difference. The land thinned out. The Frontier had been settled, or re-settled after the old world had fallen. Sure, there were still ruins, remains and relics of the old world there, but they were the outlier. People had torn them down, replaced them with new buildings, new life, even if it was a simple one.

Not here. The ruins still stood, clogging up everything. Overgrown trees and vines had reclaimed much of them.

The ground here was barren, so it couldn't be reclaimed, couldn't be grown upon, and so the only way to live was to scavenge through what remained of the old world.

And scavenge people did, some making a good living by pulling out what was still useful, and trading it back east. Emma's lighter, her pistol, a few other items were all pulled from The Scraps. But there was a limit to what could be scavenged and reclaimed. It wasn't infinite. The City had turned factories back on, had started old processes anew. Out here, there was only what remained, and what remained was petering out.

It didn't stop people from living out there, a meager life if there was one.

"You saw them, right?" asked Billy, suddenly. They had ridden a few hours, firmly inside The Scraps now.

"Of course I did," said Emma, keeping her voice low. "I'm not blind."

"Aren't you worried they're going to attack you?"

"Why would I worry about that?"

"I've seen at least a dozen eyes watching us from ruins."

"It's easily double that," said Emma. "And that's only what I've seen."

"Aren't you worried about them sniping us from the shadows, and taking everything?"

"No," said Emma. "No one out here is a predator. They're here because they've had everything taken from them. If they were going to shoot me, they would just do it. But they won't. They're afraid of me."

"Where are we headed?" asked Billy. "Or are we just passing through?"

"We're keeping our eyes open, Billy," said Emma. "On the

way to the Wastelands."

"But you don't have rad pills," said Billy "You can't—"

"That's what I'm keeping my eyes open for," said Emma. "You think I'm an idiot?"

"No, of course not," said Billy. "Maybe a little reckless."

"I think I'm doing just fine."

"I have my doubts," said Billy. "Agatha is still out there."

"She was headed the opposite direction," said Emma. "Trevor didn't mention her, and now there's a whole shit-load of City troops in the area. I'm not worried about her."

"You're not worried about Agatha?" asked Billy. "Fucking Christ. A ranger? Sure, I get it. They can be played. Hell, we just played one. But not Agatha. You're not going to trick her by throwing a bullet in a campfire."

"We don't even know why she came back down here," said Emma. "It could be for a dozen different reasons."

"Who's we? Got a mouse in your pocket?" asked Billy. "She's after *you*, Emma. Not a doubt in my mind."

"Why? Because of you?" asked Emma. "She gave you up years ago. Did you even exchange words after she left us?"

"No," said Billy. "We never talked again. But it doesn't mean she gave up on me."

"Really?" asked Emma. "Because you could have fooled me. You're lucky she didn't cave your fucking skull in after what you pulled. Hell, you're lucky *I* didn't cave your fucking skull in."

"I'm not a child," said Billy. "I made my choices."

"Giving up Agatha because you wanted to fuck some barmaid is quite a choice, I'll give you that. Especially when you had to have known that she'd find you out."

"Did you ever wonder why I did that?"

"Wonder why?" asked Emma. "It's not like it's a great fucking mystery. You were bored, and some random girl struck your fancy. It ain't complicated."

Billy sighed. "That ain't it. Okay, maybe it's partially it. But yes, of course I knew Agatha would find me out. But I was tired of her. I was tired of how she acted about me. How she thought she owned me. Especially when it didn't work the same going back the other way."

"You could have tried talking to her about it," said Emma. "Instead of just fucking around."

"Do you *remember* Agatha?" asked Billy. "She wasn't much for talking things out."

"Fair enough," said Emma. "Still doesn't mean that she came down from the north just to get you back."

"Just because she left doesn't mean how she felt changed at all," said Billy. "She thought she owned me then. She still thinks she owns me now. Even if I'm dead. Especially now that I'm dead. Because I can't even stop her. And she's coming for me. And for you."

Emma kept her eyes open. It had been many years since she'd been out in The Scraps. She'd come out here more when she was young, enough to make a nest egg. It bought her the pistol, and after that, everything was much easier. And then she left the scavenging for someone else.

She wasn't worried about any of these scavs attacking her. At least not directly. But it was still dangerous as hell out here. Buildings routinely collapsed, barely standing after decades and decades of abuse and neglect. And they wouldn't attack her, but they'd prey on other scavs in a moment, if they knew they could get away with it.

They rode for hours, passing empty land and ruin in

equal measure.

"I wonder if it's still there."

"Wonder if what's still there?" asked Billy.

"That," said Emma, as they passed through a ruined square, and a towering statue came into view. It was massive, standing 30 feet tall. It didn't stand alone, as numerous smaller tents, shacks, and lean-tos had been built around it. Only the head and shoulders of the statue could be seen now.

"If anyone will have any information about rad pills, Jonas will."

"Who the hell is Jonas?"

"An old friend."

"Bullshit," said Billy. "You don't have any friends. And how do you know he's still alive?"

"I don't," said Emma. "But I'll find out soon enough."

A few men loitered outside the conglomeration of shacks, sitting around a meager fire, burning inside of a trashcan.

"Jonas here?" asked Emma, riding up to them. Neither of the men answered. Both looked thin, with sunken cheeks. One whittled with a stub of a knife.

"Speak English?" asked Emma.

"Give me something to eat," said the first. "And I'll answer your question."

"You got any rations to spare?" asked the second. "And I'll tell you."

Emma looked between the two. "Neither of you makes a compelling case."

"Come on, lady," said the first. "We're starving."

"Yeah," said the second. "We haven't eaten in days."

A third voice came from past them. "Take the food you

were going to give them, and give it to me." Jonas appeared, his left leg trailing behind him. He wore a dark robe, his feet wrapped in bundles of cloth. A wild mane of white hair covered his head.

"Jonas, what the fuck?" said the first man.

"Shut up, Larry," said Jonas. "She wasn't going to feed you. Emma bargains hard. Hey, Emma. Long time no see."

"Jonas," she said.

"Let's take a walk," said Jonas. He walked away from the camp, down another small street of ruined buildings. His leg trailed behind him, but if it hurt, he didn't show it.

"Never thought I'd see you again," he said. "But telling from the smell coming off your horse, you won't be here long."

"No," said Emma. "How's your leg?"

"Oh, terrible," he said. "Every step is on broken glass. But I'm not about to stop moving just because it hurts."

"I could have sat and talked," she said. "I've been on the horse for hours."

"I have to walk every day," said Jonas. "Or it only gets worse. I know you're not much for small talk. What do you need?"

"Rad pills."

"So you are going to the Wastes, then."

"Yeah," said Emma. "I don't have pills."

"We haven't seen any in years," said Jonas. "Worth more than my weight in gold, if we found any. The City would pay dearly for them."

"You talk to them?"

"A ranger shows up, once a year or so," said Jonas. "Friendly enough. I'll be dead before they start re-taking

The Scraps."

"So you don't know where any are?"

"Well," said Jonas. "That's not entirely true. I know where some *might* be."

"If they're worth so much, why haven't you investigated?"

"Because I don't want to be shot," said Jonas. "And I'm not going to send someone else to get shot either."

"Shot by who?"

"Auto turrets."

"No such thing."

"Bullshit," said Jonas. "I saw them myself."

"You saw guns that aimed and fired by themselves?" asked Emma. "Where?"

"There's a bunker," said Jonas. "Old world. Who knows what's inside. But I saw a man cut down by the guns, and all he did was get too close. There might be rad pills inside. There might be all kinds of things. It's hard to say. I'll give you directions."

Emma eyed him as they walked. "What's the catch?"

"I want a cut," said Jonas. "Whatever you don't use."

"What if I use it all?"

"Then so be it."

"Where's the bunker?"

"I'll draw you a map," said Jonas. "But be careful approaching. I'd say it was thirty feet, and then boom, it opened fire. And there were no warning shots. Buddy of mine was ripped apart. Lucky it wasn't me."

"Lucky is the word I would use to describe you."

"Let's head back. I'll get you the map," he said. "Can you throw me a couple rations, too?"

"Is that part of the price?" asked Emma.

"No," said Jonas.

"I'll give you them if I get back," said Emma. "And I haven't been chopped in half by those auto turrets of yours."

"Fair enough."

*

The bunker was where Jonas said it was. Emma didn't get there until near sunset. It was a hard ride, over mixed terrain. Old asphalt covered some of the path, switching back and forth between muddy paths and stone. She had to dismount multiple times to make sure the horse didn't kill itself. The bunker was tucked behind old fence, half fallen down, with barbed wire running over. She guided the horse around the wire, and saw the bunker, a massive thing, a cement dome emerging from the ground, crumbling stone stairs leading down into an alcove. A metal door sat there, plain and unassuming.

"Looks like a trap to me," said Billy.

"No one asked you," said Emma. She tied the horse off and crept closer. The light was fading, but she still saw the gun emplacements. Jonas had tipped her off, and they were easy to spot. They were recessed, but she saw the barrels. But she wouldn't have needed Jonas' info to spot them. Two massive signs were posted on either side of the door.

WARNING

STAY AWAY

LIVE GUN TURRET

She eyed the twin signs. They weren't identical. Hand painted.

Emma grabbed a rock and threw it in between the two turrets. No movement, no gunfire.

Hmm.

Emma threw another, but nothing still. She drew her own weapon, and stalked down the stairs that led down into the alcove. She reached the bottom, and the guns were above her now, the metal door 40 feet away. Inching forward, her eyes stayed glued to the two guns, waiting for them to move. She would dance backwards. Jonas had said they were fast, but she trusted her instincts over some automated guns. How fast could they be?

Inch by inch, Emma crept forward. She moved closer and closer, right up to what she reckoned was thirty feet.

No movement by the guns. She inched ahead, ready to dance, to dive backward out of the range of the guns if necessary. But there was nothing.

Emma moved farther, pushing past the imaginary boundary, but still, the guns didn't fire, didn't move. She narrowed her eyes in the dimming light. No movement at all.

Something wasn't adding up.

She walked forward faster now, still waiting for any movement, but there was none.

And there wouldn't be any. The guns were dead. If they once fired, they weren't firing now. She moved past the ensconced guns to the metal door. The signs, upon close inspection, looked amateurish. Someone had hastily scrawled on two pieces of scrap, and glued them to the walls.

Emma tried the door. It swung open, the hinge lightly squeaking.

More stairs greeted her, but also electric light. She had

seen it in The City, but almost all the power grids had been destroyed for a hundred years. This place had its own electricity. She stepped inside, her pistol leading the way.

The stairs led farther down, and she moved quietly. The sound of voices reached her from below, a couple people arguing about something.

Her descent led her to another door, metal, same as up top. The hinge didn't squeak on this, and she went inside, peeking in.

The door opened up into a massive area. She didn't know what it once had been, but now it seemed to be a lounge of sorts. Two old men sat across from each other, playing cards in hand.

"You've been sandbagging me the whole time," said one.

"I've been doing no such thing," said the other. "And I refuse to play if I'm going to be treated like this—"

"Put up your hands," said Emma, pointing her gun at them. They both jumped at the sound of her voice, and then threw their hands into the air, dropping the cards.

1

"Please don't shoot us," said the first man.

"We're not armed," said the second. Their cards fell around them like leaves. A small wooden table sat between them, stacks of impromptu poker chips sitting on top. They both wore simple clothes of long sleeve shirts and wool pants.

"Who are you?" asked Emma, her gun dancing between them.

"We're nobody," said the first man.

"Your names," said Emma. "What are your names?"

"Edgar," said the first man. Edgar was taller, thinner, with thicker hair.

"Daniel," said the second. Daniel was shorter, and stouter, and was bald except for a thin horseshoe of white hair.

"Edgar and Daniel," said Emma. "Why are you down here?"

"We're just trying to live, ma'am," said Edgar. Fear filled both their faces. Neither were a threat.

"You can put your hands down if you promise not to shoot me," said Emma.

"We don't have any guns," said Daniel. "Unless you count the ones out front."

"They don't fire," said Emma.

"We disabled them before we came in here," said Edgar. "Couldn't get them to turn back on."

"How the hell did you do that?" asked Emma.

"Traced back their electrical systems and fried them at the source," said Daniel. "Whoever built this place didn't expect for the ground wires to be accessible, but that was probably, what, like a hundred, two hundred years ago at this point—"

"Alright, alright," said Emma. "Has no one else tried to get past the guns?"

"We don't know," said Edgar. "No one else has made it this far. Aside from you."

"Guns are scary," said Daniel. "And automatic guns are even scarier."

"Plus this place is hard to get to," said Edgar.

"Anyone else here?" asked Emma. "Or is it just you two?"

Edgar and Daniel exchanged a quick glance.

"Um—"

"Don't lie to me," said Emma.

"There's more of us," said Daniel. "They're farther below. We're the lookouts."

"You're doing a bang-up job," said Emma. "Take me to

them."

"Please—"

"I'm not going to kill you," said Emma. "But I need to see the rest of this place. I told a friend I would."

Edgar and Daniel shared another glance.

"Alright," said Daniel. "I'll take you to Lucille. Follow me."

Emma followed Daniel as they left the big open space, and went through a metal door, one of a handful on the outside of the room. It led to stairs, still more stairs.

"How far down does this place go?" asked Emma.

"Hard to say," said Daniel. "Couple miles, at least. We haven't explored everything."

"Why not?" asked Emma.

"More guns," said Daniel. "We don't want to tempt fate."

Emma thought about Jonas' words. She wondered if those guns guarded more supplies.

Another set of stairs, and another metal door, and it brought them to a smaller hallway, cross-secting with another hall, and they turned left, and another cross-section, and they turned right. Emma took notes in her head, in case she had to find her way out. Or fight her way out. She had holstered her pistol, but her hand still hadn't left her hip. These two old men didn't seem like fighters, but they had survived this long. Something didn't add up.

They passed more hallways and more doors, and Emma saw others inside open rooms, sitting on beds or chairs. Some wrote, others read, and Daniel led her to yet another door. He knocked, once, twice.

"Lucille," said Daniel. "It's me."

"Not now, Daniel," she said. "I'm busy."

"It's urgent," said Daniel.

"What could be urgent?" she asked.

"We have a visitor," said Daniel. "She's here, with me. She's armed."

A silence from the other side of the door.

"Is she a threat?" asked Lucille, although Emma thought it strange she'd ask while Emma stood there.

"Not at the moment," said Daniel. "She just wants to talk."

Another beat of silence, and then the metal door swung open. An aged woman stood there, maybe fifteen years older than Emma herself, thin, wearing simple clothes similar to what Daniel wore. Her white hair was shaved short. She held a slim journal. Her silver eyes considered Emma.

"Are you alone?" asked Lucille.

"Yes," said Emma. "Aside from my horse. I left it up top."

Lucille studied her for a moment longer, and then nodded. "Come on in." Lucille gestured inside and Emma entered. Lucille closed the door behind them, and Emma found herself in a small room, with a bed in the corner. A small desk sat opposite the door.

"Would you like to sit?" asked Lucille.

"No, you can have the seat," said Emma. "I don't mind standing."

Lucille simply nodded and sat down, a careful effort as she fell slowly into the chair. She again considered Emma.

"You wanted to talk?" asked Lucille.

"I'm Emma," she said, extending a hand.

"Lucille, but you already knew that," she said. She took Emma's hand, a soft grasp and then release.

"A friend who lives in The Scraps said there were supplies here," said Emma. "He said he had never made it past the guns, but that it was worth investigating. I didn't expect to find it occupied. Clearly there is something here."

"You're already here, so I might as well tell you. Yes, there are supplies here. But they're thinning. Even with careful rationing, we're still running through them pretty quickly."

"How many of you are there?" asked Emma.

"A few dozen," said Lucille.

"Where did you come from?" asked Emma. "If you were from The Scraps, Jonas would have known you."

"We came from the North," said Lucille. "There was a similar place up there. We used it as shelter, for a long time. There was evidence inside that pointed to a twin in this area. Daniel knew how to disable the turrets outside from the other location."

"Ah," said Emma. "You, Daniel, Edgar. The few others I've seen. You're all old."

"Very delicate with words, you are," said Lucille.

"I just haven't seen anyone outside of The City much older than me," said Emma. "We're few and far between."

"We lived comfortably for a long time," said Lucille. "Maybe too comfortably. We became complacent, being protected the way we were."

"What happened?" asked Emma. "Why did you move? Crossing that much open land without protection seems dangerous."

"It was," said Lucille. "We lost a few people on the way. But I would have still done it, regardless. There was no other choice. We had to go. The North was being overrun."

"By who?" asked Emma.

"A woman," said Lucille. "When Daniel say we had a

woman visitor, I feared it was her. She was taking control of every settlement. Burning and killing anyone who didn't pledge fealty."

"Agatha," said Emma. Lucille looked at her with questioning eyes.

"You know her," said Lucille.

"Yes," said Emma. "I knew her. Worked with her even, years ago."

"The younger ones told us to run," said Lucille. "Agatha was killing anyone who couldn't work. So we came here, to escape her."

Emma exhaled a hard breath. "Well, I have some bad news. She has come south. I saw her only three days ago. She passed me on the road as I hid in the brush."

Lucille shook her head. "Bad news comes in bunches. Why would she come south?"

"She's unlikely to find this bunker," said Emma. "It is out of the way, and the guns outside are fearful, at a glance."

"It's kept us safe so far," said Lucille. "But like I said, we're already running out of supplies."

"You can try for The City," said Emma. "You may make it there. They're accepting of old timers."

"Maybe when Agatha is clear of the area again," said Lucille. "But we need supplies to last us until then."

"Daniel told me there were deeper stores in the complex, guarded by more guns."

"Yes," said Lucille. "But we don't know how to get past them, and Daniel himself can't figure these out. I will not throw people into gunfire, at least not until I have to."

"Then I ain't got a solution for you."

"That's not true," said Lucille, eyeing her.

"What do you mean?"

"There's a factory a day's ride north," said Lucille. "Old world. It still has supplies."

"Who told you?" asked Emma.

"A source topside."

"They're lying to you," said Emma. "Everything has been picked clean."

"They're not lying," said Lucille. "There's supplies there. Because they used to be ours."

"Who took them?" asked Emma. "Who's there now?"

"Cannies," said Lucille. "They hit us on the trip here. Took a few of our men and our supplies."

"And you think they still have them?"

"Yes," said Lucille. "They're trying to trade them, but they haven't gotten any takers yet."

Emma stared at her. "Then what are you proposing?"

"We are unable to recover our supplies," said Lucille. "We have no weapons, and no horses. We are not able-bodied. But you are."

"You want me to go root around in a cannibal den to get you back some supplies?"

"Yes," said Lucille. "I doubt they're anything you can't handle."

"That may be true," said Emma. "But I fail to see why I should go risk my neck. You have any rad pills with those supplies?"

"No," said Lucille, breaking eye contact with Emma. "Only food, and some fuel."

"Sorry," said Emma. "I can't help you then. I need rad pills, and if you can't give me that—I have my own worries."

"Please," said Lucille. "We need help."

"I'm sorry, I really am," said Emma. "But I don't have time for this. I have wolves on my tail. I'll keep this place a secret." She went to the door and opened it. Daniel waited on the other side.

"Wait," said Lucille, her voice sharp. "Close the door." Emma eyed her. "Please."

Emma closed the door and leaned back against it. "We have the pills," said Lucille, her voice low.

"You just said—"

"I was lying," said Lucille. "I know how valuable they are. I was holding onto them until we needed to trade them."

"Where are they?" asked Emma.

"I can't show you," said Lucille. "They're past the guns."

"I thought you said you hadn't gone any deeper," said Emma.

"Daniel has," said Lucille. "In secret. He found a way. We've been keeping it from everyone else. He says there's weapons down there. Rad pills. All kinds of stuff."

"Then trade that for more supplies," said Emma. "Don't ask me to go steal from cannibals."

"Believe me, that is the plan," said Lucille. "But we need to make it 'til then. Just to tide us over. I don't know any other way."

Emma stared at her. "I could take them from you. Gun you all down and force Daniel to take me to them."

Silence hung between them. Lucille stared at her. "You could," she said. "But you won't. You would have already done it. You're not like them."

Emma looked back at her. "You swear you have the pills?"

"Yes. You can have them all if you bring us back supplies.

We need to eat. All of us."

Emma squeezed the bridge of her nose, closing her eyes.

"Okay," said Emma. "Give me the location of the factory. I'll get you your supplies. All of them."

"Thank you, thank you—"

"Thank me when I come back," said Emma. "You don't have them yet."

*

Emma heard the footsteps long before she saw the source of them, and she drew her pistol, aiming it at the sound as it approached her camp.

"Don't shoot," said Lucille. Emma saw Lucille emerge from the dim darkness, dressed in her plain clothes, picking her way through the rocky terrain, and Emma stowed her gun. Her eyes stayed on Lucille, and soon Lucille was next to her and the small campfire she'd built. "Can I sit?"

Emma gestured across the fire, and Lucille dropped down the light blanket she carried before sitting on it, softly grunting as she set her old bones down.

Emma had retreated back to the surface after her business with Lucille was settled. She didn't like the feeling of the ground above her, of the cement pressing down on top of her. She had expected to be alone the whole night.

Well, alone with Billy.

Lucille stared into the fire, silently. The crackling light of the flames made her look older than her years.

"I come up sometimes, just to get some fresh air," said Lucille.

"Do they know you do it?"

"What, come up?" asked Lucille. "I don't hide it, if that's what you're asking."

"But isn't coming up here asking for trouble?"

"It's a small risk," said Lucille. "And sometimes, you take the small risks if it means maintaining your sanity. Living inside a concrete cage may be safe, but never seeing the sun or moon, or feeling the wind—after a while, it grates on me."

"How long have you been living down there?"

Lucille stared at the fire.

"I don't know, for sure," she said. "We've only been here for a few weeks. But at the other location?" She paused. "Years. At least a decade. We didn't count the days, at first."

"How do you lose track of time like that?"

"At first, we just wanted safety," said Lucille. "You ever been up north?"

"Only a little," said Emma. "Too cold for me, even in the summer."

"It's hard up there," said Lucille. "But we managed."

"How long have y'all been together?"

"I've known some for twenty-five, thirty years."

"That's a long time."

"It is," said Lucille. "And we've lost some along the way." Emma nodded, staring into the fire. Lucille glanced up at her. "But we knew how to survive up there. Where and how to scavenge. But as the scavenging dried up, things got harder, and nastier."

"And you're not fighters."

Lucille's eyes went to Emma's revolver.

"No," she said. "We're not. And when we stumbled upon the other bunker, it felt impossible. Solid doors, hidden away, with an incredible amount of supplies inside. Completely empty of people."

"No turrets?"

"We disabled them," said Lucille. "Just like here. Only difference was that there, we could turn them back on."

"That's about as safe as you can get."

"We were on the run," said Lucille. "Some outriders had gotten wind of us, and were on our tail. We hid." A small smile lit up her face. "It was a miracle. We were safe. Truly safe. I'd never had that feeling before."

"Of not waking up scared?"

Lucille nodded. "Not worrying about tomorrow. It's all I did, for a long, long time." She looked down at her hands. "So we stayed, and we realized we could stay as long as we wanted. It seemed like there were endless supplies. And sure, it was great, knowing we'd eat tomorrow. That no one could steal from us, or hurt us. But—but after a while, I wanted to be outside again. So, I'd steal out at night. Turn off the guns, and go sit in the dark."

"And then retreat back into the cage."

"Yes," said Lucille. "The safety—it was worth it. At least that's what I told myself. But what else were we to do? I had to take care of my people."

"You could have defended yourself."

Lucille stared at her, with sadness in her eyes. "We're not wolves, Emma. Not like you. If we want to live, we have to run. We have to hide. And steal our moments with the moon, and the fire." She looked back into the campfire. Emma said nothing.

They sat together, silent.

Eventually, Lucille stirred, and pushed herself off the ground, grabbing her blanket and shaking off the dirt.

"Thank you for the fire," said Lucille. "And thank you for helping us."

Emma thought to caution her again, that she hadn't returned yet, hadn't done anything yet.

But Lucille had already walked away, into the darkness, back down into the concrete cage.

12

"Still can't believe it worked," said James, warm, next to her in bed. They had made it back to Alton, with nary a sign of the outlanders following them. The gang had celebrated with food, drink, and dancing. It was mid-morning, and her eyes were fuzzy from sleep.

"They're not smart, darlin'," said Emma. "I told you that."

"I know," said James. "But falling for that stupid bait and switch. I can scarcely believe it."

"Believe it," said Emma. "And all that loot. All ours."

"Well, gold now," said James. "Billy was smart, to line up the fence before the heist. Somebody else's problem now."

The rented bed was warm and her feet grazed against James', but then her stomach roiled, and she waited, maybe it would go away, but nope, and it seized again, and she pushed herself up, and ran to the bathroom, naked.

Her head went into the toilet and she threw up what remained of their dinner the night before. She coughed and puked again, until her stomach was empty.

"You alright, darlin'?" asked James, their pet names for each other the same.

Emma spit into the toilet. She didn't respond, waiting for her stomach to calm. Making sure it was gone for now before she answered. Because it was a complicated answer, more complicated than James expected.

The nausea confirmed it. There had been an anxiety in her for the past month, one she could put off for a moment here or there, but not for long. It kept hanging around, a question that could change their lives once answered. She hadn't had any drinks since it arose, and had been more careful than usual out on their ranges. She'd felt the sickness a couple times before, but hadn't been sure, and hadn't seen a doctor. Hell, didn't know if a doctor could help her, not unless they went into The City. And they weren't going to do that.

She didn't answer, not at first, wiping her mouth with the back of her hand. Emma pushed herself up to her feet, her body aching, and she walked back to the bed, where James sat up, watching her. He had the look on his face, one that said he knew something was up, but he wouldn't ask, because it'd only hurt in the telling.

"I'm pregnant," said Emma.

"You sure?" asked James.

"Yeah," said Emma. "Been two months since a period. Nausea in the mornings, going for weeks now. What else could it be?"

James nodded. She sat next to him, and he put his arm around her.

"I want to keep it," said Emma.

James said nothing. Only squeezed her shoulder with his warm, callused hand. She knew it was impossible. They had never discussed children, because it had always felt like an impossibility. James had thought he shot blanks. Most of the boys who grew up too close to the Wastes were infertile, and they'd assumed no different about James.

But it was more than James shooting blanks. It was about the life they lived. They did what they had to. They got by, on the wrong side of the law, even if there wasn't much law out there anyways. But neither of them was deluded enough to think it was a place to raise a child. Even if they could keep it safe, raising a kid to be an outlaw like them wasn't right. That had never needed to be said between the two.

Getting rid of it was an option. Lizzie had gone to a woman, out in the hills, who gave her a terrible medicine that tasted like chalk, and it had taken care of it. Easy enough, and fairly common. Everyone knew the score on trying to raise a child, especially living on the road.

But Emma had an itch, deep inside. She was already past forty, and she didn't have many years left if she was going to have a kid. She had pushed that urge away, and told herself it just wasn't for her. Growing up out here, scraping and fighting for every meal, for every score, it was easy to do. There were a lot of things out there that weren't for her. And a child was one of them.

But maybe it was for *them*. She and James, together.

"I don't know how," said James, finally, his voice struggling to leave his throat.

Along with that desperate anxiety, and that clawing itch, was another thought, that kept rising in Emma's mind, as the gang would camp down out in the wilderness. A thought that brought up a terrible, awful, chilling ache, deep in her guts. The feeling of knowing that what you're doing is wrong, terribly wrong, but you're doing it anyway, because you want it, so, so bad, no matter the consequences. The thought would arise, and the pain would follow it, and she would dismiss it, push it away. But there was no more time for it. It was here. It needed to be reckoned with.

"Yes, you do," said Emma.

"I do?" asked James. Emma turned and met his eyes, confused. He raised an eyebrow.

"There's a way," said Emma. "Might be the only way."

"What, retire?" asked James.

"Not quite," said Emma. "At least not the way you're thinking."

He looked at her, a realization dawning on him. "Emma—"

"What other options do we have?"

"We can't do it," said James. "It's not worth it—"

"What, exactly, isn't worth it?" asked Emma. "Raising a child of our own? Living a life where we don't risk getting shot at every other day? Having land, a house, of our own? Is that what isn't worth it?"

"All those things aren't worth selling out what we are," said James. "You know the price."

Emma stared at him. "What we are?" asked Emma. "What are we, James? You think because we wear white hats that we're the good guys? We kill and steal, just like everyone else out here. Doesn't make us any better."

"No matter what business we get into, it's different out here. You know that. Going—" He took a breath. "—going to the City is a line we don't cross. Everybody out here knows it. We handle it our way. They want to stomp everything out and take back control. Put us back where we were before, in the old world."

Emma swallowed. "And what's so wrong about that?"

"I don't know, Emma," said James. "There ain't no coming back from it. It's tossing away this life. All of it. No rebuilding it once it's done."

"We won't have to worry about that," said Emma. "Do you need to keep robbing outlanders with lousy bait and switch schemes? Stealing from other thieves? Looking over your shoulder whenever you post up at a bar?"

James took another deep breath. "I want a kid, Emma. I do. Never thought I had a chance at it, y'know. And waking up next to you every morning, in our own house, on our own homestead. The City will give it to us, I know they will. But I also know what they'll ask for it. And it won't be us paying the price. It'll be them. It'll be Billy, and Lizzie, and Elijah. They won't get no homestead. They'll get servitude working in a City factory, if they're lucky. A ranger bullet, if they're not. I don't know if I can live with that."

"Where were you born, James Burns?" asked Emma, glancing at him.

"Some shack, out in the Remnants," said James. "By a momma who didn't want me, and traded me for food to a merchant, who sold me himself."

"That sounds like a shit hand you were dealt."

James smirked. "Not ideal, no," said James. "But I've made due. I've found you, at least."

"In a better world, we could make a family and a life the way we want. Our sweat and blood on the line, and not someone else's."

"But we don't live in a better world," said James, his eyes on hers.

"No," she said. "We live in this one, where we've done what we could with what we've been given. But we can't raise a child out here. It ain't right to do it, and you know it, just like I do. And my whole life I've told myself that kind of life isn't for me, and it will *never* be." She grabbed his hand and squeezed it. "But I'm tired of that. I'm tired of things being out of my reach. Out of our reach. And if other people have to pay the price for me to finally get what I want, then so be it."

"You can live with that?"

"For our baby? For you, and me, having a normal life?" asked Emma. She looked at him, her eyes hard. "Yeah, I can live with it. I can handle it."

James said nothing. He only looked at his hands. His hands, that had pulled a gun out of holster, and pulled the trigger, many times. Covered in calluses and scars. He put them together, and he rubbed them, rasping like sandpaper.

"That's what you want?"

"Yeah," said Emma. "It's what I want."

James looked at her, his eyes hard now, like hers. "Then that's what we'll do."

13

"You should have just taken the pills from them," said Billy.

Emma rode toward the factory, where Lucille had directed her. It was a half day ride, given what she knew. The road was quiet.

"I'm not going to do that," said Emma.

"So killing a bunch of people for their stuff is better?"

"They're cannibals, Billy," said Emma. "Who the fuck cares if they die?"

"You'll care if you end up on the butcher block," said Billy. "They're fucking dangerous."

"Everything's dangerous," said Emma. "We're out in The Scraps now. There ain't no safe bets. And I'm not going to steal from old people. They're lucky to be alive. Agatha chased them down here. They'd be dead if they didn't run."

"Who gives a shit?" asked Billy. "You said it yourself. No rules out here."

"I give a shit," said Emma. "There are still some boundaries I won't cross."

Billy laughed, a deep, barking laughter, a laugh she had always hated when he was still alive. It wasn't his real laugh. That was high pitched, and scratchy. This darker laugh was only to inflict pain, to show just how stupid Billy thought you were. Because make no mistake, Billy always thought he was the smartest one around, even when all the evidence proved otherwise.

"That's a good one, Emma," said Billy. "I know why you didn't you just take the pills."

"You don't know anything about me, Billy," said Emma. "You always thought you knew everything, but guess what, you were always a fucking idiot, who would have died a dozen times over if it wasn't for me and James protecting you."

"That's bullshit."

"No, it's not. So don't go acting like you know what I'm doing," said Emma. "I need those pills, and I'm going to clear out some cannies that should be put down like the dogs they are. It ain't complicated, no matter how you mean to make it."

"Whatever you say, Emma," said Billy. "Whatever you say. We almost there?"

"No," said Emma. "No, we're not. And the asking doesn't make me go any faster. I'm keeping my ears open."

"I bet you are," said Billy. "I would too if Agatha was out there. She's going to take those ears off your head."

"I don't think so," said Emma. "Nothing's gonna stop me, Billy. Nothing."

The sun rose high in the sky, and Emma saw the first landmark Lucille had pointed her toward, an old water tower, a hole ripped in the side, any sign of paint or identification long stripped away by the weather. It hadn't held water in a long, long time.

She hadn't been lying to Billy about keeping her ears open. And sure, she was keeping them open for Agatha, because she wasn't stupid, but she doubted Agatha would come after her here. Last time she saw Agatha, she was riding toward the fort, and The City troops. If she was lucky, Agatha tried to pick a fight with them, got killed, and she wasn't around anymore to track Emma.

But Emma didn't think that likely. So Agatha was probably out here somewhere, tracking, trying to pin Emma down. She wasn't close though. Emma would bet on that.

Emma kept her ears open for the cannibals, especially now that she knew they were close.

They used to be a worse problem, the cannibals, back when the wild was a little more wild.

It was the only line you didn't cross, when she was a child, growing up. Most anything else could be understood, even if it wasn't forgiven.

But desperation pushed people there when they ran out of food and saw an opportunity. And once you crossed that line, there was no coming back. And the cannibals would use any trick in the book. They came across it once, as they were ranging, her and James and Billy and the gang.

A little girl, in the road, next to a body. Crying for help, crying for her mother.

Emma rode up front, because she always rode in the front. Her eyes and ears were too valuable. She knew trouble before anyone could sniff at it, and even if she was the captain of the group, she still took lead. She heard the girl screaming long before she saw her, but you didn't need Emma's ears to hear it. Everyone had heard it. Emma kept them behind her.

The girl sat next to a corpse in the middle of the road. The pair laid in the heart of what used to be a town, ruins surrounding them. It was the Scraps, back when the Scraps still had something to offer.

Emma stopped, a hundred feet from her. Emma sat on her horse, staring. She held her revolver in her hand, on her lap, a pose that seemed lazy at first, but Emma never held her gun without reason.

James rode up next to her, waiting, the little girl screaming in the middle of the pavement. The rest of their crew moved up behind them and stopped.

"We gonna help her?" asked James, eyeing Emma. They were an item by then, Emma's hard exterior cracking under James' sustained pressure. It helped that he was handsome as hell.

"No," said Emma.

"What do you mean, no? We gonna leave a little girl like that helpless, alone out here?" asked James. "I know it ain't none of our business, but I don't think I could live with myself, leaving her out there like that. She'll die."

"It's a trap, James," said Emma. "It's one of two things. Either that ain't her mother, and her real mom is waiting for us under cover, or that is her mom, and whoever's waiting for us put her out there."

"Who? Bandits? Scavs? Pretty low, for either of them," said James.

"Cannibals," said Emma. "Look at the girl. How come her clothes are so clean? Who the hell lives out here with pristine clothes?"

"Nobody," said James. "I don't know how you can see that."

"That little girl ain't starving, neither," said Emma. "Because this trick has worked more than once. Her momma is a cannie, and so is she."

"Jesus Christ," said James. "Feeding a little girl human flesh—" James spit to the side. "What do we do? Ain't no easy way around, is there?"

"Maybe if we go off the road," said Emma. "But they're probably ready for that, too."

"You think they're heeled?" asked James.

"Probably," said Emma. "Probably not well, though. They might just let us pass, if they see we're a threat. But maybe they want the fight. They get our weapons, our loot, and they have our meat."

"I don't intend to die in some stock pot."

"They won't cook you alive, darlin."

"Still, we should kill them," said James. "It ain't right."

"What about that little girl?" asked Emma. "We can't adopt her."

"We could drop her off at a church," said James. "They'll do her right, no matter what she's done."

"Until she kills one of the holies in the night and starts eating him," said Emma. "There's only two ways out of this. We shoot her dead, right now, and start this off. Or we turn around, and go another way."

"We gotta get back east," said James. "We don't have time to go around."

"You're a good enough shot," said Emma. "Take her out."

"You're not serious," said James.

"No, I'm not," said Emma. "But it doesn't mean I'm wrong. Any other choice is playing into their favor, putting us where they want us to be. Do I want to kill every one of 'em? Yes. But it won't help us doing that."

"So we've gotta tell the crew to turn around, and ride for an extra—what, a week?—because of this? And leave these fuckers alive, so they can massacre the next poor bastards that come along?"

"We would have to," said Emma. "But we're not doing that. We're going to do what they want and probably get ourselves killed."

James stared at her. "I was wondering if you were okay. None of that talk sounded like the Emma I knew."

"Just because I never say the rational things don't mean I don't think them," said Emma. "Let's gather the troops. We've got to have a plan."

The girl continued to scream, even as the gang clustered within plain sight of her. The little girl did as she was told, and Emma assumed the cannibals lying in wait had been patient so far. They would continue to be patient. They were being watched, everything they did.

They made a plan, and they followed it. Emma rode back to where she'd been, and then dismounted, letting James lead her horse off. He and the rest of the gang rode away, even if he did hold Emma's gaze for a long moment, telling her everything he felt with his big brown eyes.

She moved her head subtly, a slight gesture only he saw and then he turned the horses, and followed the rest of the crew, out of sight. The plan wouldn't work if the cannies could see 'em. Emma held her pistol in her hand, loose, but all she had to do was find a target and it would bark death.

The little girl still cried and wailed, her hands on the corpse in front of her. Emma walked toward her, her spurs tinking with every step, the cracked pavement below her. The girl's face couldn't be seen clearly, hidden in shadow, bouncing as she sobbed. Emma approached her. She heard her crying, but she also heard the shuffling from the buildings to her left and right, and a soft footstep coming from the building to her nine 'o clock. The building to the right had a recessed doorway, but it was empty. Ten feet away. If she was quick—

"Hey, you alright?" Emma asked.

The little girl only cried, and then looked up at Emma. Her dress was clean, but her face was pock-marked, her eyes cloudy.

Oh God.

The girl's eyes cast in her direction, but they saw nothing. She'd spent too much time in the rads, clear as day, and Emma was wrong, all wrong, and she couldn't negotiate with these folk. She moved fast then, her hips and knees still spry, and grabbed the girl with an arm and pulled her to her chest, ducking back into the alcove with her gun already up, searching for a target.

She saw one, a shadowy figure emerging from a building and she shot BANG and it fell and she saw one more and fired again BANG, both shots true, because Emma's eyes didn't miss.

No more emerged. A voice shouted out.

"Give up the girl and we'll let you go," said the voice. It was a man's voice, scratchy and hollow.

"Bullshit," said Emma. "You'll cut me down where I stand and I'll be tomorrow's dinner." The girl squirmed in her grasp, but Emma pulled her even tighter, using her body as a shield. If they had guns, they weren't as good a shot as her. The kid weighed nothing, made of paper. The girl still hadn't spoken, only continued to wail, and Emma didn't know if she had senses at all, if the combination of the rads and cannies had hollowed out all her feeling.

"We'll get you in a rush. You don't have that many more bullets," said the cannibal.

Emma put the gun up to the girl's head. "I'll take your bait from you."

"You'd kill a little girl like that?"

"Yes," said Emma. "It'd be a mercy."

"We ain't fed her any long flesh," said the cannibal. "We ain't monsters."

"Just call it human," said Emma. "You ain't dressing it up. I have an offer for you."

"What's that?"

"Let me take the girl, and I'll let you leave alive."

The cannibal laughed. "I don't know where your men went, but we got you outnumbered," he said. "And you're not taking her. She's mine. Stole her, fair and square."

Come on, James, hurry the hell up.

"It's my offer. Take it or leave it. It's the only thing I'm going to give you today."

The cannibal laughed. "You'll be giving us more than that, sweet meat."

Then footsteps, and a horde of them appeared in view, all of them charging her at once. She brought up her pistol and fired BANG BANG BANG BANG, and each round landed, each time a body falling, but there were a dozen more, and she went to reload and they were on top of her, pulling the little girl away, and they'd stick her and *sorry, James, I miscalculated* but a different sound interrupted them.

BANG

BANG

BANG

A chorus of gunfire erupted as the gang arrived, riding around and coming in while the cannibals were distracted. Hands stopped pulling at the little girl, and the horde of cannies grasping at her turned and were gunned down. A couple ran, but they couldn't outrun bullets.

Lizzie came from a building, pushing out a man. The source of the voice, their leader. He looked ragged, his skin sallow, his eyes half closed.

"This ain't right, this ain't right," he muttered. Lizzie kicked him in the back of the knees, forcing him to the ground.

"What ain't right?" asked Emma, handing the little girl off to James. "That your dumb bullshit trap didn't work on people with half a brain? That the shame you been pushing away finally is coming home to roost?"

"High and mighty," said the man. "I ain't 'shamed. It's just meat, like anything else. You wouldn't know. You've never been hungry."

"I've been hungry," said Emma. "Plenty in my life. I just ain't some lowlife monster who'd eat people." She approached him, reloading her pistol 1, 2, 3, 4, 5, 6 and then spinning the chamber home.

"You don't know, you don't kno—" Emma raised her pistol and shot him BANG between the eyes, and he fell dead.

"Ain't interested in speeches," she said. "We got 'em all?" She reloaded, 1.

"Yeah," said James. "I sent Billy after a straggler. What do we do with the girl?"

"We'll take her to the holies, let them take care of her. She's afflicted. Don't know what sense she's got. Spent too long in the rads."

"What do we do with the bodies?" asked Lizzie.

"Leave 'em," said Emma. "They can feed the buzzards."

They had taken the girl to the holies, and the monks took her in without a question. They used to sell rad pills, back when they were plentiful, before everyone realized what a resource they were. Back when there still *were* holies.

"Wonder if that girl is still alive," said Emma, muttering to herself.

"What girl?" asked Billy.

"Shut up, I wasn't talking to you."

"Why are you getting those pills, Emma?"

"What the fuck kind of question is that?" asked Emma. "So the rads don't eat me alive while I'm burying you where you belong."

"You didn't answer my question."

"Yes, I did," said Emma. "We're getting close. Be quiet."

Emma saw the factory, the tall chimneys rising into the air. It was right where Lucille had said, and easy to find. She circled the area, spiraling around, looking for signs of scouts or lookouts. But it was quiet, buttoned up. She tied off the horse a distance away, and approached on foot.

14

Emma had never been good with a knife. It didn't work like her gun did, killing anything she could see. The knife had to be guided, had to be forced, and was limited by her hands, by her arms, her wrist. It was as slow as her hands, which wasn't fast enough. A blade was never as fast as her eyes. Only a bullet could match her vision.

But she still knew how to slit throats, and she kept her dagger sharp, just in case.

She held it in her left hand, her pistol in her right, her finger resting against the trigger. If she was training someone to shoot, she woulda told them to keep that finger off the trigger, you don't know what you're doing.

But she knew, and that trigger was as good a friend as Emma had anymore, and her finger touched it elegantly, ready to fire if she came upon some cannibal predator hiding in the shadows for her.

But there weren't any waiting. She prowled around the factory and then entered, the cannibals not bothering to put up any defenses. Maybe they didn't expect any retribution. Or maybe they expected the factory to be all the defense they needed. It had half fallen apart, holes in the walls of most buildings, catwalks and metal stairs leading up and around in a maze. The sun was high in the sky, making it impossible for Emma to truly hide, at least out in the sun. But no one was out. Cannibals stayed away from the light.

She'd heard all the stories, over the years. That eating human flesh turned them into nocturnal animals, changed how they lived and breathed. That something shifted in you when you ate human meat, that you became more like an animal.

Bullshit. They were predators, sure, but that wasn't different from any human. But when you're hunting humans, you change your schedule to suit theirs. Their prey would sleep at night, and so they would be awake at night, to attack them while they slept. And they themselves would sleep during the day.

Emma peeked in through a hole in the side of the factory wall, seeing only darkness, and hearing nothing. She ducked in, crouching, her knees and hips aching, and stared into the dark, waiting for her eyes to adjust. She stayed still, and the world of shadows inside slowly grew brighter. While she waited, she listened, and heard nothing but a quiet shuffling, maybe a hundred feet away. Nothing else. But she also smelled.

And what she smelled was death, and decay, and the

stench of rotting flesh.

She squeezed the grips of her pistol and dagger, and soon the interior of the large factory space came into view.

She had stepped into a storage area of the factory, with huge metal canisters stacked on one side of the big room, with high ceilings and catwalks above her. A few of the canisters were whole, but most had rotted through. What once was the storage for the old world factory, whatever it had made, was now storage again for the cannibals. Because she saw the source of the smell.

A pile of human remains lay along a far wall. The pile was large, three or four feet high by maybe ten feed broad, and Emma thought to steer clear of it. It stank, even from fifty feet away, and she had seen many bodies before. She didn't *need* to see more.

But she walked closer anyway. A part of her needed to see the remains, to see the cost of these terrible fiends that had infested this place. Emma was tasked with cleaning them out. She would know their crimes. She would know her own righteousness.

The pile was immense, and the smell was terrible as she approached, a stink so strong she felt its presence in the air, wafting through the big room of the factory. And the bodies were barely recognizable. Spines and rib cages lay apart from each other, with bones and cartilage picked clean of most meat. Organs lay in piles, hearts and kidneys and unrecognizable pieces of viscera piled in a sloppy mess, parts the cannibals couldn't or wouldn't eat.

Emma held her breath as she examined the pile, and then she heard the shuffling noise, the same as before, but closer, and she turned, the gun pointing at the source.

But it wasn't a threat, and her finger and her trigger stayed only friends. It was alive, but it wasn't a cannibal. A packhorse stood there, tied off to a railing, a bucket of water and a bucket of grass in front of it. It softly moved back and forth.

Lucille's packhorse, it must be, and Emma saw the cart, only a few feet away from it, loaded down with supplies, tied over with blankets. The cannibals had clearly picked through it, because the blankets had been ripped away in places, and crammed back. But there was still a substantial amount of provisions, and the horse as well. Emma could leave now, take the horse and supplies, and get back to Lucille without the cannibals even knowing.

She heard James' voice in her mind, and she patted the horse on its neck, softly, and then turned, walking past the pile of remains, the dozens and dozens of innocents killed and eaten. Her blood burned hot inside her, her chest growing tight. She tried to breathe, but all she could smell was the death, the rotting remnants of people trying to survive in a terrible place, their last memory being hunted by savages. She couldn't leave, not now, not yet. Not while they still breathed.

Emma spotted the double doors that led to the next area, and pushed them open quietly. She held them quiet, held everything quiet, as she stalked the factory. She heard breath now, the calm breath of someone sleeping, and found a small office where a cannibal slept, a man of middle age, wearing clothing similar to what Lucille and her people had worn. Emma moved with quiet purpose and plunged the dagger into his throat, pushing it deep so he couldn't utter a word except for ragged gasps. He reached for his throat, and his blood splashed onto the floor as he convulsed and died.

There were more, Emma knew, and she prowled through the factory, her gun and knife ready. She didn't clean her blade, quickly finding more sleeping monsters. She killed them too, her dagger cutting them second smiles as they slept, each grasping for their precious blood. But Emma smelled the scent of death on them, saw the bloodstains on their hands, the dozens of people they had killed and eaten, and there wasn't an ounce of mercy in her. No regret as her blade sliced through their tender flesh. She left their bodies where they lay.

They didn't expect her, they didn't expect this angel of death as she moved through their home. A few were awake, but none of them saw her either, and she never had to fire a shot as she crept through the grounds of the factory. Blood pooled beneath them as she worked. Tired of the death, tired of these predators, tired of moral grays and ethical questions. She had encountered an enemy that required no thought, no doubts. They would be eradicated because that is what they demanded, what they had earned.

The factory wasn't large, and she had worked through the grounds twice over, killing every killer as they lay, their teeth stained with the blood of humans, their stomachs engorged with the flesh of their fellow man. No more, no more.

She found only adults, no children to be saved, no questions asked. It was only the monstrous remains of what used to be people, and Emma made sure that they died. If only she could transport them all to the Wasteland, where she could bury them all right next to Billy, where they could be sent to Hell to rot for what they did in their desperation.

Emma found death in the factory, and she only left more. An hour had passed by the time she returned to the pack-horse, the factory as quiet as she had found it. She holstered her pistol and wiped her dagger clean on a stray cloth. She took the horse and tied it back to the cart, pushing open the overhead door that the cannibals had used to bring it inside. Emma led the horse back to her own, where it still waited, the sun still overhead.

"That took less time than I expected," said Billy.

"I'm not done yet," she said, and rummaged through Lucille's supplies. She would have to understand. Emma found it, a small jug full of pink fuel, salvaged from somewhere up north, and she returned to the factory. She doused the remains in the fuel, and then poured herself a path. Emma lit it with her lighter and backed away, watching the bodies go up in flames. She threw the rest of the jug in, hoping it would be enough to burn them all.

The two horses waited for her as the smoke rose from the factory. It was catching.

"You goin' ta tell me what happened in there?" asked Billy, as Emma mounted her horse, taking the packhorse by the reins, and riding away from the factory, back toward the road, toward Lucille and the underground bunker.

"No, I don't think I will," said Emma. "We got what we came for. We can get the rad pills now, and we can be on our way."

"On our way?" asked Billy. "If you say so, Emma. Why do you need the rad pills?"

"Goddamnit," said Emma. "I told you, I don't want to fucking rot from the radiation."

"That's what you said before," he said.

"And it's still the goddamn answer," said Emma. Her blood still burned inside of her, even after killing all those murderous cannibals. She couldn't rid herself of the anger. "Stop fucking asking me."

"I won't ask again," said Billy. "Promise."

Emma rode in silence, back toward Lucille, leading the packhorse, which pulled their cart full of supplies. It was nearly dark when she got back. The ride had been easy. As she approached the bunker, something felt wrong. The air felt different.

"Something's wrong," she said.

"I would say so," said Billy. "That's what I've—"

"Shut up," said Emma. She was close to the bunker now, and she had kept her eyes and ears open for anything. She never turned it off, never let down her guard. It was ingrained in her, a skill once learned never forgotten. There had been no sign of trouble, no errant tracks, no sound of ambush or sign of a waiting trap. But something was wrong. And she was too old to ignore her gut. She led the horses away from the road, into a small copse of trees. They'd be invisible from the path. She dismounted and went in on foot, aware of every sound she made and every line of sight.

The path was hard without a horse, but it would have been just as hard trying to get that cart up there. Maybe there was a back way—she pushed the thoughts aside. She focused on her senses.

As she worked her way toward the bunker, there was nothing amiss. Maybe her hackles were raised for nothing. Still, she kept her hand near her pistol as she hiked. Emma got to the entrance quickly enough. Once there, she took her time and surveyed the area with the dying light. Nothing amiss, nothing she could see or hear. Her senses told her everything was fine, but still she felt something wrong.

She circled back around to the entrance to the bunker, and everything seemed normal. But she trusted her gut and kept her hand near her pistol. She went inside, and listened, and heard nothing. She crept down, farther and farther into the bunker.

Emma came to the first big room, where she had found Edgar and Daniel earlier. No Edgar, No Daniel.

The tension pulled harder inside her. Something was wrong.

Turn back now. Something's wrong here.

No, she needed those damn pills. She moved through the massive room, and went farther down, down stairs, into hallways, remembering the path to Lucille. The place was quiet now, all the doors closed. What the hell had happened here? Where was Lucille, and everyone else?

She followed her memory back to Lucille's room, her pistol out now. She knocked on the metal door, waiting for an answer.

"Come in," said a voice, impossible to recognize through the thick bunker door.

Emma opened it, hinges squeaking.

Lucille stood inside, her eyes full of sadness. She wasn't alone.

Agatha loomed behind her, her gun to Lucille's head.

15

"Hey Emma," said Agatha, her huge pistol aimed squarely at Lucille's head. "It's been a while." Agatha was dressed like she always dressed, in a dark duster and a beat up hat, with three holsters belted around her waist. Her pants were denim, and worth more than Emma could imagine. She was tall, and broad, and strong, without an ounce of fat on her. They'd always said that Agatha was one of those old statues, come to life. Made of marble.

The doors throughout the bunker opened, and more of Agatha's crew poked their head out behind cover, some holding more of Lucille's people. Emma was caught out in the open, she was dead, there was nothing she could—

"Agatha," said Emma. "Didn't think I'd ever see you again."

"Time makes fools of us all," said Agatha. Emma thought to pull up her pistol, one shot, directly into Agatha's forehead, she didn't miss—

"I wouldn't," said Agatha. "You don't want little old Lucy here to pay the price, do you? 'Cause even if you do get me, you can't get us all. And all of them will die."

"What do you want?" asked Emma, her gun still at her waist, her finger still caressing the trigger, not lovers, not yet.

"We really doing this?" asked Agatha, her lips curled into a thin sneer.

"What do you want, Agatha?" asked Emma, again.

"Fine," she said. "I want Billy's body. And you're going to give it to me."

"I don't know what you're talking about."

"Don't play stupid," said Agatha. "You should know better. It'll get you *and* them killed. I want Billy's body back."

"Why would I do that?" asked Emma. "After everything I've already been through."

"'Cause you don't want to die, and you don't want these innocent folk to die," said Agatha. "'Cause I will kill them, Emma. Every last one of them. A bullet each. You'll be last."

"Why do you want it?" asked Emma, staring Agatha in the eyes.

"I have my reasons."

"That's a hell of a thing to say," said Emma. "You fuck off, start your own company, leave us in the lurch, and expect me to accept 'I have my reasons'? Go fuck yourself."

"Says the woman who sold out her gang, so she could live fat and happy—"

"I did what I had to," said Emma. "To make sure my son

had a good life. Why do you want Billy back, when you left him in the first place?"

"Because I love him, Emma," said Agatha, her eyes cold, her voice dead. "Alive or dead, I still love him. Never stopped."

"You sure have a funny way of showing it," said Emma. "Normal folk don't abandon their loved ones for years."

"Billy was never the easiest one to love. I think you could agree."

"You don't get to decide now that you still love him," said Emma. "Not after what he did."

"You don't tell me who I love, and who I don't," said Agatha. "I love him, and he doesn't deserve this."

"You know what he did—"

"Yeah, he killed your son," said Agatha. "And you killed Billy right back. Seems fair to me."

"Ain't nothing fair about killing an innocent when they got their whole life ahead of 'em. Fair is taking Billy out to the Wastes and burying him deep enough that he gets sent straight to Hell."

"I won't allow that."

"I rightly don't give a shit about what you'll allow," said Emma. "I'm not giving you his body, no matter what you say."

Agatha rolled her eyes. "You never could take the easy way, Emma. You give me his body, and everyone walks away. Nobody else dies. Aren't you ever tired of all this dying?"

Emma stared at her, her face unflinching. "No."

"I could just kill you," said Agatha. "We've got you out-number—"

"You'll never find him," said Emma. "Without my help. I

hid the body, 'fore I came here."

Agatha sighed and pursed her lips, reading Emma. Everyone shuffled around, and Emma heard one of Lucille's people sadly sobbing in the background. Lucille stared at Emma, her eyes full of sadness and frustration. They begged Emma to give up the body, to make this all go away. Emma ignored her.

"Fine," said Agatha. "Have it your way."

She fired her pistol BOOM and the heavy round blew Lucille's brains against the wall.

Everything then happened very fast and very slow.

It was always the advantage that Emma had, that she saw so well, and processed things so quickly. As Agatha's finger pulled the trigger, Emma heard the movement, and was already thinking as the shot fired and Lucille died. Before Lucille's body began to slump, Emma was already moving, raising her pistol to fire at Agatha. Agatha would be moving too, and Emma didn't know if her shot would land, not where she aimed it, but it would do its job, and keep Agatha busy for a moment, because there were at least a dozen other wolves in these hallways with her, and she would have to kill them all.

There were two doors behind Emma, one to the left, and one to the right. Both had members of Agatha's gang, and she would have to kill one or both to have a chance at this.

Emma fired as Lucille's body crumbled BANG and the shot hit Agatha in the side, Agatha moving enough to keep it from killing her outright. But she moved to the side, and Emma had already moved back, firing once, twice BANG BANG into the two rooms, first one then the other, and one of the two gang members fired BANG at the same time, and

Emma felt the bullet carve a slim path of fire through the meat of her right bicep, but both her shots found homes and the two men fell over, dead. She ducked back into one of the rooms. Edgar sat inside, slunk back into the corner, his face full of fear.

Emma reloaded her pistol 1, 2, 3, and then grabbed the pistol from the man on the floor. She would need all the firepower she could handle, at this point. She was never as accurate with her left hand, but she was in close. It would do. She'd been in the room for fifteen seconds, and any longer they would pin her down. She glanced out fast, ducked back in, and then slid out to the far wall, the close quarters a blessing and a curse.

Two shots rang out BANG BANG as she moved out, but they aimed where she'd been and they missed, and she fired four more shots, two from each pistol, BANG BANG, BANG BANG. She faced a four way intersection of hallway, and the first two shots took a man and woman ahead of her down, both rushing to get position but then caught out of it. The third and fourth took out two men rushing in from the right, one getting caught in the eye, and the other in the chest. Both fell dully.

Two more rushed out from the left and Emma fired BANG BANG, a shot from each pistol, and both fell. She pushed back toward the exit, finding two more men, both holding a member of Lucille's people as a shield. Emma fired once BANG, and took one of them in the head, but the other fired, and Emma dove, rolling her way behind the two stack of men she'd killed. The lone remaining man fired BANG BANG BANG BANG, and each of the rounds thudded into the bodies she hid behind. More ran up behind her and she turned and fired, sprawled on the ground, hiding behind corpses. BANG BANG BANG BANG. Two shots landed on each of them, but she had to fire more, had to be sure, she had no cover from them. Emma dropped the extra pistol, and reloaded her own, 1, 2, 3, 4, 5, 6, even as more shots thudded into the corpse she hid behind.

BANG BANG BANG BANG BANG BANG. They dully landed, but the body worked as an adequate shield, and she pulled the man's pistol from his hand. She heard the man reload, and she stood up, her knees screaming but she ignored them and pushed forward. The man was awkwardly reloading while still trying to hold one of Lucille's people close, and Emma raised and fired. He fell, dead.

That was a dozen people, all dead, and Emma waited for movement, for more men to rush her. It'd taken less than a minute, the shootout, but it had felt like hours in Emma's mind. She took a deep breath.

"Any of Lucille's people—yell out if there's a man with you," said Emma, waiting for a response. But there was none. Only Agatha, then.

Emma slid the borrowed pistol into her waistband and reloaded her own, 1. She listened for movement, any muted sound over the ringing echoing in her ears from the gunshots inside the small space. But nothing. Agatha still hid inside Lucille's room, then, nursing her injury.

Emma walked back toward Lucille's room, stepping over the corpses of Agatha's gang. All of them were hard men, but they died the same. Emma glanced around the corner, down the tunnel that led to Lucille's room, but it was clear, and she raised her pistol, keeping it trained on the open doorway. Any movement, and she would fire.

She slowly advanced. She pictured Agatha ducked on the other side of the door, holding her side, blood pouring through her fingers. Emma let her wait as she advanced slowly. She took the closest room, holding Lucille's doorway. Emma's bicep burned, blood trickling down her arm, but she held the pistol aloft. She'd hold it all day if she had to.

"You brought this upon yourself," said Emma.

"Oh, go fuck yourself," said Agatha. "You always did think your shit didn't stink."

"I never got myself into trouble I couldn't get myself out of," said Emma. "And I was never cruel for no reason. You didn't have to kill Lucille."

"Was that her name?" asked Agatha. "Who gives a shit? Old timer was going to die soon, anyway. You *let* her die."

"You killed her over a dead man."

Agatha laughed. A deep, dark laugh, the only laugh she'd ever had. "That's rich, coming from you. A dozen of my men. Those cannibals these old folks sent you after. God knows how many more, just this week. But I've seen you kill dozens, back in the day, Emma. And I didn't even ride with you that long! How many more have you killed? How many men have you killed with that damn impossible aim? With those hawk eyes? How many? You call me cruel. Nothing crueler than sending a man to hell over an accident."

Emma's breath burned, her heart aching.

"Are you gonna come out here, or am I gonna have to come in there and dig you out?" she asked.

"Oh, don't you worry," said Agatha. "I'll take my medicine."

Emma heard Agatha shuffle around inside, pulling a second pistol, most likely.

Agatha came through the doorway, her guns out, her face full of frustration and pain.

Emma shot her twice BANG BANG, and she fell, and she died.

16

They cleaned up the bodies.

Emma helped the rest of Lucille's people carry them out. She took what she could from them.

"What do we do now?" asked Edgar.

"What do you mean, what do you do now?" asked Emma. "I've got your supplies back. You can live off them. If you take Agatha's crews horses, you can make a pretty penny. Honestly, I'd ride east, and try to make a go of it in The City. They'll take you in."

"Lucille made all the decisions," said Daniel.

"I'm sorry that's she dead," said Emma. "But there's not much more I can do for you. You'll have to make your own decisions."

"We'll have to talk to everyone," said Edgar, looking at

Daniel. "Maybe we can decide together."

Emma stared at them. "Lucille said there were rad pills, down below. She promised me them if I brought back your supplies. Past more guns."

Daniel looked at her then, confused. "Lucille told you?"

"Yes," said Emma. "And I did my half of the deal, and brought you the supplies. I'll even help you get them down here, if it comes to that. But I need to know where the guns are. Lucille said that you made it past them."

"Oh, uh, no—no," said Daniel. "We couldn't." He averted his gaze now, his hands grasping. Emma narrowed her eyes.

"Daniel, you're a bad liar," said Emma. "Are you telling me Lucille was lying to me?"

"No," said Daniel. "She wasn't—wasn't lying. Here, I'll take you. But you can't let the others know. We'll wait until they're all asleep, okay? It shouldn't be too long. It's getting late, anyway."

Emma led them to the packhorse, and their supplies. Edgar showed her an easier path, one that the pack horse could handle, pulling the cart. Billy was right where she left him.

"You killed her, didn't you?" asked Billy, after Edgar and the rest of Lucille's people had taken the supplies, ferrying them inside. The sun was almost set now. Emma piloted her horse back up near the entrance of the bunker, where she had slept the night before.

"How did you know she was here?" asked Emma.

"Just a feeling I had," said Billy.

"Yeah, I killed her," said Emma. "And all the men she brought."

There was a long pause. "You get your pills?" asked Billy.

"Not yet," said Emma. She left him and the horse there,

and went back down into the bunker, finding all the people organizing the supplies, talking over what was left. They all saw her enter, and avoided her gaze, all except Daniel. He walked over to her, hurriedly.

"Everyone will bunk down in a few hours," he said. "You can wait in my room, if you want."

Emma waited, walking past bloodstains and bullet holes. Daniel showed up an hour or so later.

"I'm sorry," he said, closing the door. "For that. But the rest of them, they can't know."

"Why not?" asked Emma.

"They would hate me," said Daniel. "Worse, they would hate Lucille. And I don't want that, especially not now. I know she's hidden things from us before, but I always trusted her. She always had good reason. And I don't expect this is any different. That's what makes this so hard." He stared at her. "We're going to do what you suggested. We're going to try and make The City. None of us are particularly good riders, but we're not going to have a better chance."

Emma waved him off. "Daniel, what was Lucille hiding? Are there not guns? I need those pills—"

"No, there are guns," said Daniel. "She was hiding the fact that I was able to get her past them. She made it down below."

"Well, what's down there?"

"I don't know," said Daniel. "I couldn't go with her. The guns can be only be turned off for a short amount of time, and we both would have been torn apart by them coming back up. I had to make sure it was safe. So only she went down there."

"And she didn't tell you?"

"She told me there was nothing down there," said Daniel. "But she was lying."

"How do you know?"

"I knew her for thirty years, Emma," said Daniel. "I could read her like a book, after so long. There's something down there, for sure, but for some reason, she didn't want to tell me. Not then, at least. Maybe, after some time, she would have said something. Maybe she was waiting for when the time was right, or when we really needed whatever's down there. I don't know. But there is something. Her eyes didn't look that way for nothing."

They waited for everyone to settle down for the night. A few hours passed, and Daniel led Emma out, down a hallway, and then another, then another. Only the sound of their footsteps followed them.

"You can find your way back, right?" she asked.

"Yes," said Daniel. He stopped. "Do you see it?"

He pointed. They stood at the end of a long hallway, with a door halfway down. Emma followed his finger and saw the small black box that jutted from the ceiling.

"Doesn't look like a gun to me."

"Don't be fooled by it's looks," said Daniel. "It'll kill you, just the same."

"How do we get past it?"

"We can't," said Daniel. "Only you can. Here." He crept toward the door ahead of them on the right, his eyes never leaving the gun emplacement in the ceiling.

"I thought you've done this before."

"I have," said Daniel. "Doesn't change the fact that it scares the shit out of me." He moved forward until they reached the door, with the gun still sitting motionless. Daniel pushed the door open, and Emma followed him inside. The room was small. A computer sat inside. With power. The screen blinked.

"Holy shit," said Emma. "I've never seen one with power before."

"Not even in The City?"

"I'm sure they had them, but I never saw them," said Emma. "More precious than gold. And it's just sitting in here."

"It controls the gun," said Daniel.

"You know how to work it?" asked Emma.

"Yes," said Daniel. "I've been practicing. It's not that complicated, honestly. But I can only turn off the gun for minute long increments. And then it starts again. I've tried to keep it off, but it won't work. I think something's broken in the system."

"It's old world," said Emma. "Means it's been running for a hundred years."

"I don't know if that's true," said Daniel. "Might have just cycled on when we came inside. Either way, I don't think it's operating optimally. But it'll do what we need."

"How do I tell you to turn them off again?"

"You don't," said Daniel. "It only scans ahead of it. So just stand behind it. I'll be waiting at the end of the hall, and see you. I'll go and turn it off."

"You sure it only scans forwards?"

"It didn't shoot Lucille," said Daniel. "So, pretty sure. You ready?"

"Ready as I'll ever be," said Emma. "Lucille gave you no clues about what's down there?"

"No," said Daniel. "But she went down unarmed, and

came back unscathed. So there's nothing dangerous down there, at least."

"What the hell could be dangerous?" asked Emma. "The place has been abandoned since the collapse. It's not like there's wild dogs down there."

"I don't know," said Daniel. "You only have a minute when I flip the switch, so hurry." He looked at her, raising his eyebrows.

"Do it," said Emma. Daniel typed something real quick on the keyboard.

"Okay—it's done. Go."

Emma nodded at him with a final glance and left the control room, heading toward the gun emplacement, hurrying. If it would shoot her, it would shoot her, but it stayed still as she approached it, only thirty feet away. She saw the barrel now, recessed inside, and it was thin, a small caliber, but then again, if it shot out a dozen rounds with perfect accuracy, it wouldn't matter if it was a small caliber. A person would die just the same.

Her eyes stayed on it as she hustled past. Daniel had exited the control room, and stood at the end of the hallway. He raised a hand, and Emma raised one in return, before turning away.

The hallway turned to the right, and then she was presented with stairs, leading down, and then turning, and she went down.

The stairs went down and down and down, turning many times over. They ended at a door, and Emma went through, her right hand not leaving her hip, ready to draw her pistol. The door led to another hallway, with another door at the end.

How many damn hallways are in this cursed place?

She walked to that door, her footsteps echoing off the tiled floor. This one was different though. Heavier, thicker, with a more complicated latching system. Emma began to analyze it, but realized that it lay unlocked. Lucille had already done it, and Emma simply pulled it open. It opened into a small antechamber, but there wasn't a door leading out. It led into a central area, open, ringed with more doors, similar to the ones above. No sign of anything strange. Lucille's footprints dotted the dust. She had explored the space herself, but wherever she hadn't stepped was steeped in grime. What had she discovered down here?

Emma retraced her steps, starting with the left most door. She went from room to room, looking for a sign of anything, attempting to piece together the same thing Lucille must have, before Agatha had shot her. She looked, but all she found was death.

Emma found only bodies. Many of them. All of them long, long dead, all the flesh rotted away, long ago. They laid in beds, or sat on couches, or sat at desks. Some of the rooms were clearly living space, others offices.

But Daniel was right. There was no danger down here. Lucille had found a mausoleum. A few dozen people living down here, after the collapse. Waiting for word that it was safe. There were other computers as well, and books, and notebooks. Emma was sure someone would find all the records interesting.

But Emma didn't give a shit about the old world. She needed rad pills, and that's what she looked for. Lucille said they were down here, and Emma scoured for them, looking through cabinets and drawers and pockets. There had to be a doctor's office, somewhere in here, some medicine of some kind. Surely, in a place like this, there'd be rad pills.

But there was nothing. No medicine left, no food, no nothing. And Emma realized that the people down here, all of them, had starved to death. They had been waiting for things to blow over, and over never came. And they waited, for God knows how long, and help never came, and things up top never changed. And they died.

As she searched, Emma's guts roiled inside her, a deep, darkening feeling of frustration and anger, and she threw open boxes and searched for pills, tiny white pills that she used to laugh at as a young woman, back when they were plentiful, but she'd been so stupid, and Lucille hadn't lied to Daniel. Because there was nothing down here. All of this for nothing. Emma wanted to scream, but she sat down instead, her breath heaving.

Her hands went to her face, and tears welled in the corner of her eyes, but she forced them back.

No. No time for sadness.

She took a deep breath, and forced all of that frustration and anger and rage and futility and pushed it down inside, and stood up, and walked back the way she came, out of the lower facility and up the stairs. She reached the gun emplacement again, and sure enough, Daniel waited at the other end of the hallway, sitting on the ground.

"Daniel," she shouted and his head perked up. He pushed himself off the floor and went into the control room. He re-emerged a moment later, and hurriedly waved her down. She hustled back to him.

"Well?" asked Daniel. "What's down there?"

"Death," said Emma, looking at him briefly, and then

breaking eye contact.

"What? What do you mean?" asked Daniel.

"There are bodies down there, Daniel," said Emma. "And that's it. Lucille wasn't lying. Maybe if you dig into their computers, you'll find something interesting. Old information, stuff like that. But there's a bunch of people down there, all starved to death. Been there since the collapse. No food. No supplies."

"Oh," said Daniel. "Well, the information might be useful. Especially to The City."

"If you can get them here, they'll probably reward you. Can you lead us back? I need to sleep tonight. Get an early start."

"I was going to ask you," said Daniel. "Will you come with us? We need protection, and if this stuff is valuable, you'll be able to cash in with The City. And without the rad pills—"

"I'm not interested in gold," said Emma. "Not anymore. My business is in the opposite direction." She stared at him with dead eyes, and Daniel only nodded.

"I'll lead us back then," he said, and they went through the maze of hallways again, back to the entrance.

"I'm sorry about Lucille. I truly am," said Emma.

"Are you sure you don't want to come—"

"I'm sure," she said. "I'm going to sleep up top. I'll be gone in the morning. Take care," she said, and Daniel only nodded.

Emma left the bunker for the last time, finding her horse and Billy where she left them. She grabbed her bedroll and laid it down without a word. Too late to start a fire. She'd deal with the chill. She laid down, her body weary, when

Billy's voice interrupted her.

"Did you get your pills?"

Emma laid still, feigning sleep.

"Did you get your pills, Emma?" he asked again.

She sighed. "No," said Emma. "There were none inside. They lied to me."

"So, we're turning back, right?" he asked. "Going back to The City."

Emma laid there, quiet. Finally, she answered. "No," said Emma. "We're heading out into The Remnants tomorrow."

"Is that right?" asked Billy.

"Yeah, that's right," said Emma. A silence, and Emma closed her eyes, trying to sleep. She drifted away and then Billy's voice woke her.

"Why were you getting those pills, Emma?" he asked, the same damnable question, again.

"I told you."

"Yeah, I know," said Billy. "But you lied to me."

"No, I didn't."

"Yes, you did," said Billy. "You said you were getting those pills so the radiation won't eat you alive out there, in The Wastes, which it surely will."

"I didn't lie—"

"You said you were getting the pills, so it'd keep you safe from the rads. But that was a lie. Because obviously, you didn't need those pills at all. We're still going out there, you and me, aren't we?"

Emma laid there, quiet for a moment. "Yes."

"So it didn't really matter if you got them at all, huh? Pills or no, we were making the trip. Only difference is, we'll be leaving two bodies out there, instead of one."

17

There was no line drawn where The Scraps ended and The Remnants began. No border town, no trading post. The occasional ruins of The Scraps got thicker, and the vegetation grew heavier, and Emma knew then that she was in The Remnants.

No one lived in the Remnants, at least not in heavy number, and not for long. It could serve as temporary shelter. When she was young, she had come out here to hide, before she met James, before she'd organized. It served well, because there were so many hiding places. The buildings still stood in The Remnants, far enough out from The Wastes that they weren't knocked down by the blast. But the rads were so bad that no one stayed there for long. And from what Emma had heard, the rads had only gotten worse.

Everyone always said they'd fade with time, not get stronger. Something was wrong. And she didn't have the pills. And despite what Billy said, she wasn't running a suicide mission. She'd get in, bury Billy's body, and get out. Maybe she'd get a little sick, but she could handle it. It was a price she was willing to pay.

There was no more wilderness, only what used to be city. The buildings rose high above her, and continued on, past the horizon, what was left of what was a massive metropolis, a name no one said anymore. The towers stood empty, every single scrap of anything valuable taken long ago. Much of it was discarded, when people realized the rads had stuck to everything inside. Salvaged metal and scrap had passed its curse to anyone who had bought it, even after it was melted down. After a while, people abandoned what was left to the elements. It wasn't worth the sickness or death.

But left alone, nature had taken back The Remnants. Vines, trees, and brush had overtaken medians and roads and grown up and over buildings. Some buildings still had clear facades, but most were covered in vines and bushes, and the concrete below her feet had crumbled in places from the sheer pressure of all the plants growing up and through it. No matter what man built, it couldn't withstand nature.

The plants weren't the only thing that had returned. Animal life was much more abundant in The Remnants. A deer back in The Frontier was a rare sight. Almost all were shot on sight, a source of valuable meat. Even squirrels were rare, but harder to kill, and slightly more numerous.

But out here, even in the middle of the ruined city, Emma heard the sounds of footsteps and rustling. Of animals picking through the greens, of hawks diving and scooping up rodents. A deer stood in an alley as she passed, snapping its head up at the sound of her and her horse. It sprinted away, down the alley, away from her.

Emma wouldn't hunt here, though. God knows what poison the meat contained. They all had learned that lesson long ago. Anyone who ate anything from The Remnants got sick. The rads had sunk into the land, somehow. Maybe the folks in The City could fix it. Emma hoped they could.

"You sick yet?" asked Billy.

"I feel fine," said Emma. "Thank you for your concern."

"You won't feel fine for long," said Billy. "Won't be long before you're puking up your guts."

"It was all rumor, Billy," said Emma. "Everything I heard had always said the rads would die out as time went on. Bet people are saying it's worse just to keep people out of The Remnants, so they can have the scavenge for themselves."

"It's possible," said Billy. "You ever see someone die from the rads?"

Emma paused. "Yeah, I have."

"Rot from the inside out," said Billy. "Most god awful thing I've ever seen. Person just—just starts to fall apart. Everything keeping 'em together just fails. Skin falls off, and they start bleeding everywhere, from their fingernails, and their gums, and their eyes—"

"I just said I've seen it before," said Emma. "So, for the thousandth time, you can just shut up."

"It's not too late, Emma," said Billy. "There's still time to turn back."

"After everything I've gone through?" asked Emma. "You think I'm going to turn back now, when all I've got in front of me is The Remnants?"

"You're not free and clear yet," said Billy.

"Like Hell I am," said Emma.

"You've still got a wolf on your tail," said Billy. "And you know it."

"If he knows what's good for him," said Emma. "He stopped following me long ago."

The street was empty as she rode. She pushed the horse carefully. They were close, and she didn't want it injured now. There wouldn't be any replacement horses out here. The ruined city was massive, so big that Emma couldn't see the end. The sun was high in the sky when she heard the noise.

It echoed, the sound bouncing off the dilapidated buildings, echoing between the parallel city streets. The sound was something she'd never heard before, a growl, a yell, a scalding screaming noise, coming from some creature in The Remnants. It stole her breath from her, and an unfamiliar sensation arose in her. Fear.

She stopped the horse in its tracks at the sound, trying to locate it. The ruined city was quiet then, everything doing the same as she was. Freezing, waiting. Trying to find out where the predator was. Because Emma didn't know what the hell made that noise. But she knew it was a predator.

And then the sound echoed one more time, louder now, a raucous growl, filled with instinctual rage and bloodlust. And then nothing more. Emma still didn't know what made that noise, but she knew why, somewhere deep inside. The predator had killed.

The sound came from ahead of her, somewhere, but it was impossible to tell where, the geometry of the buildings making it hopeless. She had no experience tracking in this place, and an anxiety grew within her. For the first time in her life, she couldn't rely on her hearing.

"That sounds like a nasty critter, don't it?" asked Billy.

Emma said nothing, only tapping the horse into movement again. They rode silently, and Emma listened for any trace of the beast. They traveled for an hour, Emma hyper-aware of everything around them. She pictured a prowling thing, stalking them from the ruins, a thousand different places it could hide, waiting in the shadows for them to get close, and then leaping on them, too fast for a bullet.

Nothing struck at them from the dark, but Emma had been right. The creature had killed. The prey's body laid in the road. Emma pulled her pistol at the sight of it, and cautiously walked the horse close, listening for any sign of movement. Could the thing be laying a trap?

She held her breath, her gun ready to swing in any direction and lay thunder down on whatever stalked the ruined city.

But nothing.

She dismounted and approached the dead animal. It seemed small from afar, but up close, it was bigger than anything she'd ever seen before. The deer in most of the west were small, and fast, the only ones which would survive for long, with the meager supply of food and the active hunters that killed anything slower than a bullet.

This thing was massive, bigger than her horse, with a huge rack of antlers that came two feet off its head. It wasn't a deer, but something similar. Its throat had been ripped open, a massive bite wound on its neck, a pool of blood centered around its head. The killing blow. The predator had latched onto its neck and torn out its throat, and it had died quickly. Catching it and wrestling it down would be hard for anything. It must have weighed at least a thousand pounds. At least, it had.

The predator had eaten a considerable portion of it. Its entire midsection was hollowed out, its ribcage on display to the world, broken through, to get access to the innards. Its guts had been pulled out into the street, and its soft belly consumed, along with a large segment of its intestines. Almost all the meat on the outside of the creature had been ripped away. Emma couldn't imagine the appetite necessary to eat all that flesh, hundreds and hundreds of pounds. The beast must be enormous. The smell from the dead animal overwhelmed her, and Emma backed off, getting a fresh breath.

"Never seen anything like that before," said Billy. "God Almighty."

"All kinds of things out here," said Emma. She mounted her horse again, and holstered her pistol. The predator had fed now. Animals only attacked when hungry, or when cornered. The memory of the beast's howl still lingered in her mind.

They rode through the ruined city for hours, the sun setting in front of her. Emma's eyes ached by the time it crossed past the horizon. She pulled the horse into a massive building, cutting her way through hanging vines, and leading the horse through a broken doorway. It led to a huge lobby, dilapidated and falling apart. Plants sprouted through the floor tiles and hugged the interior desk. Emma pushed deeper inside the building, darker and darker, until the sun didn't penetrate. She pulled food from her bag and fed the horse. Neither of them would be eating anything out here.

She ate, a full ration. Looks like she'd have enough supplies. It was only a few more days of riding, and then she'd bury Billy, and this would be done with. She could move on with her life.

"You think we're safe here?" asked Billy.

"Yeah, we're safe," said Emma. "That thing won't be hunting for a week, after all the meat it got off that big deer thing."

"It's an elk," said Billy.

The picture book, from the library. She had taken Thomas there, and he had picked out the picture book, and she had read it to him, it had a drawing of an elk inside—

"I guess that's right," said Emma. "An elk. First time seeing one."

"Does a dead one really count?" asked Billy.

"It counts enough," said Emma. "Just a couple more days, Billy. Just a couple more days."

"Couple more days 'til what?"

"Don't play stupid," said Emma. "A couple more days, and I'll have you buried deep where you belong. And you can finally get your punishment."

"Do you really believe that, Emma?" asked Billy. "You think because you bury me out in The Wastes, that I'll get sent to Hell?"

"That's what the old timers believed," said Emma. "And I don't have a reason to doubt it."

Billy laughed, his sneering, dark laugh. He laughed hard, and long.

"You're not that stupid, Emma," he said. "Believing what those stupid old fucks believed. Ain't nothing out there but death."

"That's what you would say," said Emma. "Doubt you're too excited about heading off to Hell."

Billy laughed again, the same laugh.

"I know you think that bothers me," said Emma. "And it does. A little. But if you think it's going to stop me, you've got another thing coming. Ain't nothing gonna stop me, Billy. I'm going to get you sunk down into the cold, hard ground, and I'm gonna turn around and head back to my life. And you're damn annoying laugh won't keep you outta Hell's clutches."

Billy was silent at that.

Emma bedded down and slept.

18

The fire burned high. Emma stood as close as she could bear, the heat almost burning her. She watched her son disappear inside the pyre, the smoke and flames engulfing him.

She didn't cry. Emma only stared, her eyes blinking away the smoke. A yawning pit of sorrow was open inside of her, and everything fell into it. She didn't want to burn her boy and watch him turn into ash as it flew into the sky, and resettle on the ground, and become a part of the land. She wanted to hold him and keep him close to her forever.

But The City had come and picked up his body, and they had gone through all the normal funerary rites. James had taken the lead on it all, on organizing when it would happen, and everything else.

She didn't cry. All her tears had left her in the days after his death, all her rage and anger enveloped by such a horrible sadness, such a deep, sucking agony that ate her up inside, a depressive cancer that absorbed her, cell by cell, until she was nothing but pain. She sobbed into the bed, wave after wave of grief, James doing all he could to comfort her. She cried until her face hurt, until she choked on her sorrow. Then there were no more tears left, but still her sobs wracked her body.

But as her son burnt in front of her, her rage rose again to the surface. It had been there, been there the moment Billy had ambushed them in the middle of the night, neither of them armed, and had shot the first thing he'd seen in the house, thinking it was Emma or James, not their little boy, who had woken up to the slight noise in the dark and was investigating, no concern or worry for danger. Thomas had walked out into the living room and had been shot in the chest by Billy's heavy pistol. The shot had woken her up.

She had cursed herself, silently, for sleeping through it all. They had grown soft, living within the protection of The City. At first, she hadn't slept at all. The familiar noises of the west were gone, replaced by the sounds of traffic from the road, only a few hundred feet away. The sounds in the night would jolt her awake constantly, her heart thumping in her chest, reaching for a gun that wasn't there. Part of the deal with The City meant carrying no weapons, not even a varmint rifle. That was one of the hardest pills to swallow when she had built her life around being able to defend herself.

But as time went on, the switch inside her mind flipped, and she could enjoy life there. Able to sleep soundly, able to *feel safe*.

The shot had woken them both up, and they found

Thomas in the arms of Billy, dead already, dead instantly, a five-year-old shot with that gun, impossible to survive more than a moment. Billy still held the weapon in his hand.

Emma couldn't breathe, a combination of things she couldn't imagine, she couldn't imagine because they were such a dangerous and deadly idea her mind wouldn't summon them, no matter how much anxiety or fear she still craved in her new buttoned-up life. It wouldn't broach the idea of Thomas dying, no matter what, because even the thought caused her so much pain that it could kill her. But she froze, and James did as well, their love for Thomas the strongest thing between them now, and Billy's eyes were filled with sorrow and surprise and watery with tears and he stared at them both. He had them dead to rights now, armed with that hand cannon, with five bullets left. Enough to take them both out with ammo to spare, but he didn't fire at them. Didn't raise his pistol at all. Just stared at them, and then ran, not saying a word.

Emma didn't think to go after him, not at the moment, even with the burgeoning explosion of rage inside. The sadness, the deep and dark void that filled her was too much, and she went to the body of her son, and she held him, and she cried.

The void was still there, but it subsided, subsided enough for her to feel that rage. The priest said his words, and everyone gave them their condolences, again, more comfort that she didn't want. And they went home, to the empty house.

James tried.

That's what she loved about him, was his endless effort, at anything they did. He didn't give up, he persisted, but in this, she just wanted him to stop. Stop trying to comfort her, stop trying to talk to her about Thomas, to just stop. Because just the sight of James reminded her of him.

Thomas looked like him, his warm brown eyes the same as James, their ears flaring the exact same way.

They went home to the empty house and Emma felt the rage boil up inside her, a great heat that flared up through her body and settled in her chest, and every breath came out like dragon's fire, and she saw Billy's face now, Billy who they had left behind, who they had sold out to The City, who had sneaked his way inside the limits and killed their son and fled like a thief in the night.

She went to their barn, and went to her horse. Healthy and strong, livestock given to them by The City, as long as they kept it up. She groomed him. He had been born and raised here, but he was tough, and he could withstand a ride out into the Frontier, as long as she took care of him. She rooted around in the barn, finding the saddlebags, and filled them with supplies, with food and with tools. Emma knew what she had to do.

"What are you doing, Emma?" asked James from behind her. He was the only one who could ever sneak up on her.

Emma paused. "Leave me be, James. Please." She kept her back to him.

"You can't leave, Emma," said James. "You know that."

"They won't even notice—"

"They will know," said James. "And they won't let you back inside The City. And especially being who we are. They won't make an exception. Not for you. Or for me."

"He killed him, James. I—" she exhaled, the empty breath that held back her words. "I can't let that be."

"Killing him won't bring back our boy."

"He can't be allowed to live," said Emma. "It ain't right. There are some things that are unforgivable."

"He was coming to kill us, Emma," said James. "He saw Thomas in the dark, and thought it was one of us—"

"You think I don't know that? You think that makes me feel better? That knowing if we hadn't done what we did, if we hadn't given Billy a reason, that Thomas would still be alive?" asked Emma. "Cause it don't. I'm the reason he's dead, James. *We* are the reason he's dead."

She turned around to look into his eyes. Into Thomas's eyes. "I thought you would understand that more than anything."

James stared at her with those big eyes, not an ounce of anger in them. Only sadness.

"You think I wasn't angry?" asked James. "That I wasn't upset? Course I was. But when we came here, I made a change, and I'm going to stick with it. Does Billy *deserve* to die for what he did? I don't know. Maybe. But nobody gets what they deserve in life. Some assholes live like kings their whole lives and never see a drop of misery. Some people work their asses off and get nothing. Just the way it is."

"I can't—I can't keep on knowing he's out there, walking around. Maybe he feels bad about it. I saw the look in his eyes. But it ain't enough. It will never be enough, and he gets to live into old age? And you'll say, oh, but he'll feel guilty." She took a deep breath. "I don't want him to feel guilty, James. I want him to be dead. Thomas didn't get his life. Billy doesn't get anymore of his."

James looked down. "If you leave, they won't let you back in. That's it."

"That ain't true," said Emma. "I can ask the Marshall to

hunt him down. He's already wanted."

"And you think he'd grant the request?" asked James. "And he'd let you kill Billy?"

"I don't know," said Emma. "Maybe. But I could go out, kill Billy, and come back. And we can have our life again." Emma felt him soften then, an unspoken empathy that she only had for James. He would say yes, allow her to leave without a fight. And that's all she wanted. She didn't want to fight with him. She still loved him, loved him more than anything else that was left in the world.

But it would need one more thing. She went to him, and embraced him, wrapping her arms around him, softly rubbing the back of his head, the soft fuzz where he kept his hair shaved, and he melted in her embrace.

"I promise," she said. "Please, if you love me, let me do this. I will come back, and we can try to put our life back together."

"You swear?" he asked, his voice a whisper in her ear.

"I swear."

A sudden jerking nausea woke her up.

Emma rose out of her bedroll in the dark, her stomach seizing inside of her. She jumped up to her feet, the abrupt feeling urgent and awful, and she ran to the side of the room she was in, leaning a hand against the wall as she threw up her dinner, the bile burning her throat and nose. Her stomach seized, and she vomited again, whatever was left, and the feeling hurt bad inside, and she puked again, even though there was nothing in her stomach, only stomach acid coming up through her throat and sinuses.

She took a deep gasping breath, forcing back this sudden tidal movement of her innards, running to her canteen, taking a small sip, hoping the water would soothe her. At least calm her guts.

She waited to see if the water would come up again, but after a few moments, it stayed down, and she took another cautious sip, her stomach aching inside of her, her throat and nostrils burning.

Emma caught her breath, taking more sips of water, the fleeting thoughts of her dream floating through her mind.

Billy's laughter interrupted them. The dark, sneering laughter.

"Bet you wish you had those rad pills now," said Billy, his voice alone with her in the dark.

19

Emma didn't sleep anymore that night. She sipped water, and it stayed down, and she considered that a victory. But it was still hours until dawn, and she sat there in the dark.

Less than 24 hours, and the rads were already inside her. Sure, the nausea could be something else. Could just be those old memories riled up her system.

But she didn't believe it. The radiation had gotten stronger out here. She had spent weeks here when she was young, and she hadn't gotten sick at all, only feeling it a little at the tail end of it. It scared her enough to get out, to head back to the frontier. The rumors were true.

She didn't have any rad pills.

As she sat there in the dark, she heard noises. The buildings rattled as the wind blew past them. She could feel the tall building she sat in shake above her. She had sat and watched them sway as a young woman, waiting for one of them to give out and fall over, but they never did. They were probably designed with the movement in mind, she had decided, but it still didn't keep from her picturing the buildings collapsing like a stack of dominoes, right on top of her.

But there were other noises, too. The sound of footfalls in the dark, of muffled sprinting, as the pads of whatever paws that great beast walked upon, softly stamped its way through the empty city. Emma had thought that the elk it had eaten would be enough food for days for that thing. That it would rest, and Emma would be out of its territory before it needed to hunt again.

But it moved in the dark, which meant one of two things. Either it was bigger than she thought, a massive beast that needed an incredible amount of food to persist—or there was more than one of them. Neither option thrilled her.

She sat quietly in the dark, her stomach aching, and the sun slowly rose, a dim light filtering into the building. She packed up her things and loaded her horse, and led it back out onto the main road. The road that would lead them to The Wastes.

Emma moved with haste as they got back on the street, her hand never straying far from her pistol. Every sound she heard was a potential attacker.

"Something's following you, Emma," said Billy.

"No shit."

"It sounds big," said Billy. "Might want to turn around, while you still can."

"I'm not turning around," said Emma. "You should know that by now."

"Lost your dinner, too," said Billy. "Bet you wishing you had those rad pills, now. Still thinking you're going to make it out of this? It worth all this, Emma?"

"Shut your cursed mouth," said Emma. "I'm not turning around until you're on your way to Hell. You won't stop me, no matter how much you babble."

"But what else do I got, Emma?" he asked. "You took everything else from me. You took me under your wing when I was barely a man, told me everything would be okay with you. Taught me how to kill, betrayed me, and then killed me yourself. And now you're damning me—and you expect me to be quiet? You're lucky I'm not screaming loud enough for that damn beast to come over here and finally kill you."

"Only thing I took from you was the burden of your guilt."

"Emma Burns, deciding what's just, and what's fair. A tale as old as time," said Billy. "Deciding who lives and dies. I shouldn't be surprised. Same shit your whole life. Always thinking you're the arbiter of good and evil, the ultimate judge."

"Shut your fucking—"

"No, Emma, no," said Billy. "I'm not done, and you can't keep me quiet. I'm sorry, I really am for killing your boy. I didn't mean to. Now, killing both of you, and leaving him alive—is that a better fate for him? I don't know. Never knew my folks neither. But I didn't kill him to punish you both. I only wanted you."

"You got me," said Emma. "If that makes you happy."

"Naw," said Billy. "Ain't been happy in a long time, and being dead ain't changed anything. I'll have to make do with you rotting on the inside."

Emma tried to push away the idea of the radiation eating at her insides, but the thoughts kept intruding. Her stomach growled for food. She hadn't taken in any calories in over a day, and her body was craving fuel. She grabbed some rations from her bag and ate them quickly with one hand, still keeping the other close to her gun.

An hour went by, and Emma thought that maybe this time she would keep the food down, but then her stomach roiled, her guts churning, some process inside being disrupted by the poison she was absorbing, and the half-digested meal came up. She leaned off her horse and threw up, the vomit splattering on the ground. She puked desperately, letting it all come out, not fighting it. After surge after surge from her guts, she breathed again, wiping her face with a handkerchief. She took another sip of water, and then another, and it stayed down.

At least she could still drink.

"Getting hungry, huh?" asked Billy. "It's only going to get worse. Wonder if it'll feel like a blessing, when your stomach stops grumbling at you. It's a desperate feeling, you know, that hunger. But soon it'll go away, because the rads will kill whatever's inside you that wants food."

"Shut your damned mouth, Billy," said Emma, her voice low.

"Turn around," said Billy. "And I'll never speak again."

Emma continued forward, trying to ignore Billy. She kept the horse as fast as she could risk, with the unsteady nature of the road beneath its hooves. Multiple times, the horse would take a step and the road would crumble beneath it, and she and it would have to adjust quickly. Leg trouble for the horse out here meant death. Still, they made progress. They would move in a straight line, as quick as they could away from the creature. She didn't know how far it roamed, but a day's ride would take them out of its habitat.

The road rose ahead of them slightly, and as Emma crested the hill, a straight line solution was no longer an option.

Her worries from early that morning, of the swaying buildings, hadn't been so far-fetched. A huge tower had fallen over, its great mass covering the entire street, crushing everything underneath it. But that wasn't all. It had toppled multiple other skyscrapers, cascading out of view, hidden by the other buildings. But she couldn't continue straight, not without going on foot. Not an option, not with the horse and Billy.

Emma doubled back, and turned north, the only option she had, the south blocked by the river. She would head north and cross back west as soon as she found a road that wasn't blocked by the series of fallen towers.

Then she heard it.

She'd been listening hard ever since they started that morning, her ears at constant attention, more than normal, every single sound that passed through her questioned and interrogated, making sure it wasn't a great beast stalking behind her, ready to ambush. But there was nothing, nothing since the sounds from the night before. She had hoped that they crossed out of the habitat of that thing, out of its hunting grounds.

But she'd been wrong, because she heard the same soft padding, a slight sound that some wouldn't have heard at all. But Emma heard it, along with the creaking of the tall buildings that still stood.

She pushed the horse harder, harder than she should,

having to hope that the road wouldn't crumble beneath its hooves. Emma hadn't seen the creature, but she didn't want to fight it. Would her pistol even hurt it? The gun would damage it, surely, but could she kill it? They had encountered a bear, long ago, a massive thing, when they ranged, and it had taken dozens of rounds to finally put it down, and it had killed two of them before they had stopped it. Whatever this thing was, it was larger than that.

She pushed the horse, and it galloped, but the soft footfalls of the creature following them was still there, underneath the sound of hooves, and she hastily looked down each street, looking for a clear road, but the cascade of towers had taken out block after block. If she knew where she was heading, she could make a plan.

Emma rode hard, looking down each street, covering blocks quickly, dodging around brush and trees that had pushed up through the road, past debris and trash, looking down street after street.

Blocked.

Blocked.

Blocked—wait. Emma pulled back on the horse and turned it down the street. A building did block the road, almost a mile down, but she spotted a way through. A concrete barrier had blocked out a small corridor. The horse would fit.

To make the turn, Emma had to slow down, and the footfalls of the creature got louder, and Emma looked backward, and the thing broke cover now. It must have been running inside of buildings, flying through broken open windows and doors, watching her as she rode. It burst from the double doors of a building, its fur flattening against the constraints of the frame.

Emma had seen nothing like it. It was massive, running on four legs, over eight feet long. Emma couldn't estimate its weight, but would have guessed a thousand pounds. It was orange, with dark stripes, a great cat. She tried to summon its name from the picture book, but she couldn't. It sprinted gracefully, every step a careful decision as it charged after her.

But something was wrong with it. Its body bulged, and its teeth were slightly too large for its mouth. Its muscles jutted strangely, and strange growths sprouted from its neck and from under its arms. Tumors. Emma couldn't imagine the animal looking like that naturally. It was bigger than normal. It needed the extra food.

The radiation. The rads have mutated it.

But its eyes were unchanged. Emma looked back, and their eyes met each other, and Emma saw a kindred spirit.

A killer.

Emma turned and urged the horse as hard as it could sprint. She could maybe kill that thing, if she hit it in the eye, but she would only take that shot if she had to. Running was a better bet, at least for now.

The horse galloped hard, its hooves smashing into the ground below it. They got closer and closer to the small tunnel through the collapsed building, a thin corridor of concrete that was only big enough to let her and the horse through. Maybe only barely, but enough. And not big enough for the beast that followed her.

And it followed her. It sprinted hard and fast, and made ground on her quickly. The monster had tracked her for miles, and it would see this through to the end. It knew only the hunt, and it would bring down her horse, and then kill her where she stood, faster than a bullet.

The horse ran hard, harder than it had run before, and the small tunnel was right there, only a moment away, and they would be safe. Emma heard the creature's breath behind them.

And then the road crumpled beneath the horse's hoof, and it fell, its legs scrambling in the air, trying to find ground, a few dozen feet from the tunnel. Emma flew from the horse's back, rolling as best she could. She felt a rib break when she hit the ground, and a spark of pain from her side as a piece of debris sliced her.

The horse whinnied on the ground, struggling. The beast sprinted past them, slowing down in front of the tunnel. It turned and faced Emma, and roared.

20

The creature roared and Emma drew her gun, and the beast pounced as she fired BANG and it flew through the air. Ten razor sharp claws filled her vision as the massive creature landed on her, its claws digging into her shoulders, its huge teeth looking to sink into her neck. Her shoulders screamed with pain and she felt torrents of blood pour out of her. She moved her head in time to avoid its bite.

She couldn't move or breath and in moments she would be dead. Her gun was jammed up underneath it and she fired freely BANG BANG BANG BANG BANG, all of the rounds thudding into the torso of the great beast. The cat roared in pain right in her ear, deafening her, and she closed her eyes waiting for the thing to rip out her throat. This was the end, not some bandit or old enemy, but some mutated animal out in the nowhere, but then the weight flew off her and she opened her eyes and the monster was gone.

Emma sat up, her shoulders screaming with pain, and the blood flowed down her back, and she looked frantically for the creature, but it had scampered away into the ruins, her bullets doing enough damage to scare it off. She wasn't worth the pain.

She reloaded her pistol 1, 2, 3, 4, 5, 6 and walked over to her horse, which still floundered on the ground. It's leg was broken, and there was nothing she could do for it out here. She caressed its neck, once, twice, and then shot it in the head, and it went quiet. She reloaded, 1.

Blood flowed down her back freely, and her shoulders spiked with pain from the row of wounds the beast had given her. Emma pulled her pack off the body of her horse, and laid it out, pulling out the meager first aid supplies she had. Enough to bandage the wounds, but she couldn't see them, and she'd be working blind. She took off her jacket, a clean row of slices in the shoulders, but little blood. But then her shirt, and undershirt. The shirt was stained with blood, and her undershirt was soaked.

She pulled out stray rags, and wiped the wounds as best she could. The rags came back sodden with blood. She carefully probed them with a finger, enduring the pain as she tested how deep the slices were.

Flares of agony shot through her, but she had to know, as she carefully touched a finger. Only a couple of them were bad. The rest were superficial, and would heal on their own. She grabbed the tiny glass bottle she kept, and dabbed the rag with it, wiping at the worst of her injuries.

The pain flared up even harder as the alcohol seeped into

the cuts, but it had to be done. She forced herself to stay conscious. She wiped the wounds clean, the liquid burning its way into her. Emma grabbed another of her undershirts from her pack and tied a makeshift bandage, wrapping the fabric under her arms and back over her shoulders, up and under, as best she could. The pressure hurt even more on the slashes, but she couldn't bleed out. Not now. It would serve well enough. She dressed with fresh clothes, throwing the bloody clothing aside, and putting her jacket back on.

"I would say I looked away, Emma, but I've seen you naked hundreds of times, so you'll have to excuse me," said Billy.

Emma ignored him and pulled things from her packs, organizing them on the ground. She didn't know if it was smart to stay here for long, with that creature presumably still nearby, but she had to organize.

"This isn't exactly where I imagined I'd spend the afterlife," said Billy. "Strapped to a dead horse in The Remnants. Could be worse, I suppose. Maybe that thing will come eat me, after it's licked its wounds."

"You're half rotted away, Billy," said Emma. "It ain't coming anywhere near you."

"What are you doing?" asked Billy. Emma had picked through her things, and re-fitted the pack so she could carry it on her back. She didn't need much. She could get the rest when she came back through. Emma went to the horse, and began cutting the ropes that tied Billy to it, and pulled him off.

"I'm getting you ready," said Emma, reattaching the ropes.

"Ready for what?"

"You think I'm stopping because the horse is dead?"

"Well, yeah, what are you going to do, carry me—" He paused. "Emma, no, don't do this."

Emma attached the ropes to Billy again, and then slung him up in an impromptu fireman's carry. She held the ropes and tied them to herself, wrapping them around her waist. Billy never had weighed much, and he weighed even less now. Still, the extra weight made her hips shift. By the end of the day, she would struggle. And the pressure on her shoulder wounds burned, and she felt more blood ooze out.

So be it. Even on foot, she would get there quickly enough.

"I told you, Billy. I'm putting you where you belong. Even if I have to carry you there myself."

She left everything as it was and walked through the slim tunnel she had aimed for earlier. She emerged on the other side, the rest of the city laid out in front of her, the edge of the Wastes in the distance.

"Fuck," said Emma.

The downed building she had climbed through was not an outlier. The cityscape in front of her was ruined, filled with broken machines and fallen towers, across all the streets she could see. She would have to climb through it all.

"You sure about that?" asked Billy.

"Yeah, I'm sure," she said. She looked hard at the border of The Wastes in the distance, a blackened line of destruction, a dark storm cloud at the edge of her vision. A bolt of lightning cracked far away, too far for thunder. Her target. She could make it. She could finish this.

Emma started down. She moved around the abandoned machines, climbing over or around them, and through the ruined buildings. Her heart beat hard in her chest, and she sweat heavily, but she did not stop. She made good time as the sun rose high in the sky, beating down on her. She focused on every step, keeping her mind as clear as she could, letting her senses guide her, doing what she had done her entire life. They had protected her; they had kept her safe, and they would continue to do so.

Moving through the downed buildings wasn't complicated, only arduous. Occasionally it would be easy, with simple paths visible, but most of the times it meant climbing, stepping up, or even an occasional leap. Her joints ached with every movement. She hadn't done anything like this in a long time. The smell of Billy lived in her nostrils now, a fetid rot that would be with her until she buried him.

She hadn't forgotten about the creature, now behind her. Emma hoped it would stay that way. She had shot it five—maybe even six—times, and all of them at close range. Regardless of its size, it would have done significant damage. But clearly she hadn't killed it. It had gone off to regroup, or to nurse its wounds.

But it was still alive.

And most creatures, once injured, would know fear of what hurt them. She and her gun would have done enough damage to do that, surely. But the thought lingered in Emma's mind of the split second where their eyes met. And Emma saw no fear in those eyes. She didn't even see the capability of fear. That beast had only hunted its entire life, and it had mutated with its time out in The Remnants. What had that mutation done to it?

Had it erased its fear?

If it had, it could still follow her, and the thought stayed in her mind as she gasped for air, pushing herself hard. She was on a clock now, the rads eating away at her. Was her breath coming harder now, her lungs losing power because of the sickness in the air? Was it just her age? The questions flew through her mind and she tried to push them aside. She had her mission. She had to finish it. Billy deserved punishment. Any moments of doubt were banished by a memory of Thomas. The anger and rage could be summoned immediately to the surface.

And then a sound, distant, behind her. A scrabbling noise, of a small piece of rock or debris shifted off, falling to the ground. She had heard nothing but the city before that, but her hackles raised, and she kept her hand close to her gun.

How could that animal still be following her? Was it angry? Did it want vengeance? Did it know anger at all? Emma pushed herself harder. The more distance between them, the more likely it would give up the trail and go back to its normal hunting grounds.

But the noises followed her. They were quiet sounds, impossible to hear by most people. *Never* heard by most people. A small shuffling noise of a footstep on dusty concrete. A scattering of dirt as it was pushed to the side absentmindedly. Noises almost everyone made, even out in the west, where they could lead to your death.

"It's following us," said Billy. "Your little pop gun only bought you some time. That thing is still on your tail."

Emma only continued forward. The noises still followed her, and she imagined the creature behind her, its teeth bared, those deadly eyes still tracking her. Smelling things she never could, easily following the scent of the dead body she carried.

"Are you going to fight it carrying me, Emma?" asked Billy. "Seems like that's a losing proposition."

"No one's asking you," said Emma, through gritted teeth.

"You should save your breath for climbing up and down through these ruins. And for fighting that terrible beast, that will soon rip out your throat."

Emma didn't argue with him. He was right. If it was the rads, or just her age, maybe the lack of food, but she was struggling. Sweat dripped into her eyes and she wiped them with the back of her sleeve. She need to take a break, to catch her breath, but she couldn't stop. Slowing down would only make her easier to find. Make her easy prey.

And she wouldn't be easy prey. If she was going to die, it would be ugly and hard.

The sounds still followed her, but now they were closer, drawing nearer and nearer, the scatter of dirt, a footstep. They came apart from each other, but soon they'd be on top of her.

As she tried to mount a concrete divider that led up into a ruined building, she paused. Emma didn't have the breath. She took a deep breath, another, and forced herself up. She had to stop. Emma would pass out on her feet, and then she'd be dead, killed while she breathed into the dirt.

An ambush is what it would take. She pushed herself through the fallen tower, one of many, looking for a vantage spot, a spot where it wouldn't expect her. She had to hurry.

Emma noticed a spot, a little nook, in between a tipped over desk and a wall, half supported. She could wedge herself in there, and not be seen. If it wanted her, it would have to come through the narrow area, and she could light it up some more. It was her best chance.

"This ain't gonna work, Emma," said Billy, as she pushed herself inside the crawlspace. "Thing is going to eat you alive."

Emma said nothing back, only listening for the sounds of footsteps and movement.

There was silence for a time.

And then she heard something, heard the same sound as before, something approaching, and she pulled her pistol, aiming it at the small entrance to her cubbyhole. She would aim for its eye. She'd have it dead to rights.

The sound drew nearer.

But it was different. It wasn't the same soft padding she'd heard before.

What the hell was following her?

It was the only reason she didn't shoot.

The sounds approached, soft footsteps walking toward her. A figure peeked into her hole.

"I can smell Billy for miles, Emma. Don't know how you think you wouldn't be found. Please don't shoot me."

She recognized the voice.

Emma's eyes adjusted to the dark.

It was James.

21

"I didn't think you'd follow me."

"What did you expect me to do?" asked James. He stood there, at the entrance of Emma's hiding place. "You don't need to aim your gun at me, Emma." She dropped it, forgetting she held it, sliding it into her holster.

"I don't know," said Emma. "I hoped you would forget about me and move on."

James stared at her. "You gonna come out of there?"

"If I can manage it," she said, squeezing herself back out. Her pack and Billy's body made it hard, but she pushed herself out of the hole, sliding on her butt. She got out, and then stood there awkwardly, staring at him. He looked exactly like he had when she first met him, aside from the streaks of gray around his temples and the crow's feet around his eyes.

He always dressed the same when they ranged, in thick, sturdy pants, with a plain black belt, a white shirt, with a leather vest and road coat.

She wanted desperately to hug him, but she was afraid to touch him. He considered her, his eyes full of frustration and sadness. They stood there, ten feet apart, a world of distance.

"What are you doing, Emma?" he asked, finally. "Carrying what's left of Billy on your back?"

"That creature killed my horse," said Emma. "It was still out there, I couldn't stop—"

"It's dead, Emma," said James. "You shot it up real good. It was clinging to life when I found it. I finished it. It clears the path for us to go back."

"I'm not going back until I bury Billy."

"You won't be coming back at all!" said James. "You told me you were coming back after you killed him. And that didn't happen."

"You would have never have let me leave if I told you what I was planning," said Emma. "And I had to do it."

"You didn't *have* to do anything, Emma," said James. He stared at her for a second, and sighed, and then turned, and walked over to a tumbled column, and sat down. He looked up at her again. "You didn't have to do anything. You could have gone back to our house, and we could have lived our life again. You didn't have to leave The City, you didn't have to kill Billy, and you sure as hell didn't have to embark on this goddamned mission to bury him out in The Wastes!"

Emma stared back at him. "Would you let Billy go unpunished for what he did? For killing Thomas? For shooting him in the dark and running away like the coward he is—"

"It's not worth it, Emma," said James. "It's not worth all the pain. You think I wasn't angry? You think I wasn't mad? We were on the road together for how long? How many times did I let someone go after they hurt us?"

"Never," said Emma, breaking eye contact.

"Never," said James. "If someone crossed us or the gang, they had to pay. It was the way things were. And our eyes would go red, and we would bleed whoever did it, bleed them down to the bone if we had to. Made things right. Made things even. More than even. They send us to the doctor, we send them to Hell, right?"

Emma looked at him.

"We never let up on an enemy. If an enemy gang tried to hit us, or stole from us. If someone weaseled their way in with us and then showed their true colors. If a ranger from The City came and tried to fuck with us. What did we do? What did *I* do?"

"We killed them."

"Yeah," said James. "We did. We killed a lot of people. And after a while, it's second nature. You do it because you're *supposed* to do it. Because if you don't, you're soft. You're weak. And that makes you a target. Word goes around that you let people live. Then people can take advantage of you, and then—well, then you're dead. Puts a bullseye right on you. On us. On the gang. And we couldn't have that, could we?"

"No," said Emma, her voice just above a whisper.

"No," said James. "We had to be strong. And hell, it worked. We lived. That's a feat, all by itself. We lived long enough to be old. Gray hair, and wrinkles, and all the aches and pains in the world. What does that tell us? Tells us that being hard *was* necessary. It *was* the only way for us to survive."

"We did what we had to."

"Maybe so," said James. "But Thomas wasn't the only reason I agreed to go to The City. He was a part of it. A lot of it. And so were you. But it wasn't all of it. I wanted to stop killing people, Emma. And maybe we did have to carve a bloody path through the Earth just to survive. But it doesn't mean I wanted to do it, and if I had a chance to stop it, I would take it."

"Why are you telling me this?"

"How many people have you killed since you left The City, Emma?"

"I don't know," said Emma. "I did what I had to do."

"I've been behind you, the whole way, trying to keep up. And everywhere I went, they talked about you being back in the west. And about the trail of bodies you've left. We were done. Retired. Billy came in, shot Thomas in the dark. One death. One tragic, awful death. And you've turned around and killed how many more? How many dozens of people?"

"They deserved it—"

"I don't care what they deserved, Emma! You ain't God. You ain't justice. What did I deserve? Did I deserve to lose my wife, after I've already lost my boy?"

"No," said Emma. "But Billy had to pay. And with more than his life. I have to send him to Hell. There is no punishment on this Earth big enough for him. For what he did to us. For what he did to *me*."

James looked down at his hands. He squeezed them, once.

"I want you to come back with me, Emma," said James.

"If you go out there, the rads will eat you alive."

Emma stared at him. "They're out here, and I'm doing okay."

"It's ten thousand times worse out in the Wastes," said James. He paused. "I brought you a rad pill."

"How did you get them?"

"From The City, Emma," said James. "I told them what I was planning, and they gave me a ration."

"They know you're out here?"

"Yes," said James. "Because I want to go back. That is where our future is, Emma. A life together. No more killing."

"They won't let me back in, James," said Emma. "I knew that when I left."

"Yes, they will," said James. "I convinced them. They'll let you back in."

"How—"

"They'll let you back in, if you bring them Billy's body. They'll forgive everything. Billy was wanted, dead or alive. Rangers didn't get him, and he slipped inside and killed Thomas. They'll forgive everything, if you bring them the body."

"What will they do with it?"

"They'll burn it, Emma," said James. "Like they do with everyone."

"He doesn't deserve that!" yelled Emma. She felt tears roll down her cheeks. "He took our son from us! Am I supposed to forget that? To forgive?"

James stared at her, tears rolling down his dusty cheeks. "He took Thomas from us," said James. "That's true. But you're letting him take everything else. Everything else you had in your life, he's getting that too. Don't let him, Emma."

Emma stood there and cried, Billy's body strapped to her shoulders.

"We can go back, Emma. We can rebuild our lives. This isn't the end," said James. "Please, come back with me."

"I don't know how."

"It's easy," said James. "We go back to my horse, and we take Billy's body off of you, and we ride back together. A few days on the road, and we're back at The City. We go back to our house and forget about Billy. Just come with me, and we can get through this."

James stood again and walked closer, extending his hand. He stared at her, waiting, tears rolling down his face.

Emma stared back, her guts roiling, her heart pounding in her ears. She forced a halting breath through her lungs. She took a tentative step forward, unsure if her legs would carry her. She took another step forward, her eyes locked onto James'. She felt the tears wet her face, and she tried to blink them clear, but still she cried.

She reached his hand and she touched him, palm to palm, their hardened, callused hands touching once again. His hand was warm and dry, and he squeezed her fingers softly as they touched. She walked in the rest of the way and embraced him, holding him tight. It was all she wanted, his comfort, his touch. It always had fixed all of her problems, just being there, close to him. Emma had wanted it since she had left The City, wanted his warmth next to her.

While she was there, all her troubles disappeared. Memories rolled through her mind, through thousands of nights of fear and sadness and anger, all soothed by James' touch, and he held her tight, and she squeezed him back. She breathed him in deep, smelling the rich musk of his scent, a smell she had nearly forgotten, sense memories flooding back.

She reached down in an instant and fired her gun BANG into his foot, and James fell.

He moaned in pain, holding his foot, a neat bullet hole in the top of his boot. Blood leaked out, and James held his foot with two hands. Emma stepped back, tears still rolling down her face.

Words came from between James' gritted teeth. "Emma, what are you—"

"There is no going back, James," said Emma. "Don't let him take it all from me? But he did! How can I go back? I did it all for him, James! We turned our back on our lives! Sold out our friends! Sold our souls to The City, for some peace and quiet and a future with our child, but Thomas is dead and there is no going back!"

"Emma, please—"

"Stop, stop," said Emma. "I hoped you would have realized it, but you came all the way out here, chased me down. Please, just go back. Maybe you can move on and live the life you want. I can't, not anymore."

"You shot me," said James.

"You can still ride," said Emma. "And you can still shoot, if you need to."

"I could shoot you," said James, his voice low.

"You won't," said Emma, staring him down, her face full of sadness. "I love you, James. Please don't follow me."

Emma turned and walked away, moving through the ruined building, climbing down through the wreckage.

James shouted her name, over and over, but he didn't follow.

22

Much like the ruined city of the Remnants, there was no beginning of The Wastes. No border, no official line to cross. But it was clear that Emma had left the ruined city behind her. Had left James behind her.

The massive towers that filled the city disappeared, and even the smaller clusters of larger buildings vanished. When she only saw complete destruction in front of her, she knew she had entered the Wastes, and knew that she was close to the end of her journey.

They said it was bombs. A massive war that saw three bombs drop in a cluster, each identical, each cascading and causing more destruction. A lot of the history was lost in the aftermath. The old ones would tell her that, that they cast about as young people in the fallout, and they had to piece things together from scattered stories and found fragments of history. The three bombs that had dropped on The Wastes weren't the only bombs dropped that day, but the rest were out of her ken.

The landscape was complete and utter ruin. Everything that had once been there had been destroyed and never rebuilt. No plants grew, and no animals wandered. It had once been a city, a likely target in war, but only wasteland remained. The bombs had destroyed everything and scoured the land with terrible radiation that kept everyone away. Rad pills helped, and it was the only way to explore the land, but even the scavs left it alone, after a while. Nothing worthwhile was there.

Aside from the burial ground.

Emma walked, Billy strapped to her back. Her body hurt, broken ribs aching, and each of the eight points where the beast's claws had sunk into her shoulders burned white-hot. Infection was settling in. But there was nothing she could do about it now. She had done her best and hoped her body would fight it off. The slim line in her bicep where a bullet from Agatha had carved a path. They all hurt. A dozen ailments accrued through the journey, along with the pain her tired body carried every day, the aches and miseries of being old.

But a worry burned inside of her, a niggling thought that wouldn't go away, that told her none of that pain was the problem, not the real source of the agony she felt.

It's the rads. You're soaking in 'em, Emma. And they're eating you alive.

She walked, carrying Billy deeper into the Wastes.

"Well, hello there," said James.

He sat alone at the bar, his cowboy hat pulled down tight. The bar was some pissant place in some pissant town. She wasn't alone, not quite. She hadn't formed the gang yet, not proper. Emma had a couple people with her, to pull some jobs, but they were hired hands, that was it, and they'd all go their separate ways after they'd made their money. But she had grown to know them. And that was a part of it.

James was the other part.

"Hello there, yourself," she said, looking him over. James was young, his face clean-shaven, his eyes full of trouble, baby-faced. He nursed a small glass of whiskey. And being a woman in the west, one that went heeled, she was used to the constant attacks from men. They saw it as a challenge, seeing her with a pistol. This was before she had made a name, before they knew that Emma killed you with her eyes and never missed. And the type of men who saw her as a challenge didn't interest her. Sure, she was human, and she had her urges, but rutting with some dumb fuck outlaw didn't interest her.

But James was different, right from the start. One, he was a handsome man, with a hard face and soft eyes and a devilish smile. And he knew it. But there were plenty of handsome men in the world. It was the way he looked at her that caught her off guard, and it was the reason she talked to him at all. She knew when men saw her as a challenge, when they looked at her and saw the gun, and were already thinking of ways of how they'd get that gun belt off her.

"My name is James," he said, turning slightly toward her. He tipped his hat and pulled it back, letting loose a curl of brown hair. She didn't know if he did it on purpose, but damn, did it work. He extended a hand, slowly, open. She studied it for a second, and then grabbed it and squeezed it once. He squeezed back with the same amount of pressure, not quite a handshake.

"Emma," she said.

"Ah," he said, his eyes narrowing just a little. "Heard about you."

"Hope it was good."

"Oh, hell," said James. "None of it was good. But that don't mean I don't want to talk to you."

"What did you hear?"

"That you're getting a group together," said James. "And you're a bunch of doombringers, that will rob anybody for anything."

"Somebody been lying to you," said Emma. The bartender poured her drink, a glass of sickly sweet liquor. She took a sip.

"What's the lie?"

"I'm not getting a group together," said Emma. "Just some folk working together, for now."

"Safer together, y'know?" he said. "A lot of gangs springing up."

"There's always been gangs."

"Not like this," said James. "With The City organizing, lot of people trying to get stronger. I don't rightly blame them. But I don't want to join just anyone."

"You ask everyone that comes in if you can join up with 'em?" she asked, narrowing her eyes now.

"No, actually," he said. "I heard word of you hitting Leroy. Did you do that?"

She paused, considering. "Yeah, I did."

"Heard you killed him. That true, too?"

"Yeah," she said. "He deserved it. He kept people. Sold them to the cannies. Some things I can't abide."

James nodded. "I don't disagree. But no, I don't ask just anybody. I knew you were around, so I waited by, and here you came."

"You waited here for me?"

"I did, indeed," he said, and downed the rest of his whiskey. "What do you say?"

"Buy me another drink," said Emma. "And we can talk about it."

"You shot him, Emma," said Billy.

Billy's voice brought her back to the surface. She'd been walking for hours, her feet and knees aching, her insides burning. A dull ache had settled in her stomach, with moments where it would churn and seize before settling again. She hadn't eaten in two days, and she only sipped at her water.

"What?" asked Emma.

"You shot him," said Billy. "You shot James."

"I had to," said Emma. "He would follow me out here. And I couldn't have that. It was the only way."

"It wasn't the only way, Emma," said Billy. "He had a rad pill. You could have taken it and gone back with him. Taken me back to The City. Gone back to your life."

"Don't know how many times I have to say," said Emma. "There ain't no more life there."

"You sure about that?" asked Billy. "You're only 48, Emma. You could have lived with James for another 30 years. Made your land into something."

Emma's foot sunk into the ground, and she stumbled, and fell to a knee. Her whole body hurt with the impact, and she kneeled there, breathing hard, her vision blurring. She squeezed her eyes shut, and then opened them, forcing them wide. She pulled her foot from the small hole and stood up, taking in her surroundings. Looking back, Emma realized the ruined city was out of sight. How long had she been walking? She'd been inside her own mind. It was late in the day, and the sun was setting behind the dark clouds. But she couldn't stop. Camping in The Wastes was suicide. She walked.

"Don't you love him?"

"Yes, I love him," said Emma. "But he doesn't understand. Maybe James can just cut out the part of him that survived in the west his whole life, but I can't. I can't just go on existing knowing that you've gone unpunished."

"Death isn't enough."

"No," said Emma. "You have to rot in Hell. And there's only one way I can guarantee it. Only one way I can make sure you get justice. And James don't understand. He couldn't. He didn't make our boy. Didn't feel Thomas growing inside him. Didn't feel the pain I felt. He couldn't know, and my words wouldn't convince him. He doesn't understand, he couldn't understand—"

Pain ripped through Emma again, and she stopped and swallowed back bile. She spit to the side, and she walked.

"You've been out in these rads for hours now, Emma. Turn back now."

"No."

"It's worse out here, and you know it. If you keep going, there's no turning back."

"Leave me alone, for God's sakes, just shut up, shut up—"

The pain ripped through Emma again, and she fell to her

knees, and she couldn't hold back the vomit anymore and she threw up, torrents of bile coming up through her throat and sinuses. It burned like hellfire and she puked, and she saw red, bloody chunks of tissue coming up with the mass of bile. The rads. They were breaking her down.

"Please, Emma," said Billy. "Please."

Emma rose to her knees and stared at her hands, stained from the filthy ground. They trembled, and thin lines of blood rose from beneath her nails. This place was eating her from the inside out.

Maybe Billy was right, maybe James was right. She had pushed for days and days, and killed dozens of people, to get this far, and who knows how far she'd have to go. She would die here, fall down in the Wastes, with Billy strapped to her back, and no one would ever find them, and she would never bury Billy. This would all be for nothing. She stared back at the way she came.

She could go back. She could go back, and her body would heal. The City would let her back in, and she would trade Billy's body for her old life. James would forgive her.

Emma forced herself to her feet, and turned back, toward the ruined city, toward The Remnants, and The Scraps, and The Frontier. She took a deep breath that rattled inside her. She just had to hold together. She would walk through the dark, back into the city, and make her way back to civilization. Emma would pull herself back from the brink.

A sweet relief entered her heart, the world finally handing her a defeat she could stomach, something she couldn't shoot her way out of. Despite the terrible pain in her gut, she felt something akin to happiness again for a moment.

But then she craned her neck, back out to farther in the

Wastes, and she saw it, against the dark horizon, standing tall.

The monument. Distant, but there, a darkened silhouette. She had never seen it, but everyone spoke of it when they spoke of the burial ground in hushed whispers, a terrible marker that overlooked them all, a blackened obelisk that marked the center of the ground, and the closer you buried the dead, the darker the Hell they went.

And her heart sank, and vengeance consumed her.

She turned away from her home and walked.

23

The obelisk grew in size as Emma walked toward it. Her insides burned, her throat on fire. Every breath came through ragged chunks of flesh. Her whole body ached, her joints scraping with each step. Her body was failing.

"Turn back, Emma. Turn back," said Billy.

"No," said Emma. "I'm here, now, finally. I can finally put this behind me."

"What are you even talking about, Emma?"

"I'm gonna bury you, you son of a bitch," said Emma. "I'm going to put you in this cursed ground, and finally, finally, you'll get the punishment you deserve."

"You already punished me, Emma."

It was dark when she found him. He wasn't hard to find. Billy was never good at covering his tracks.

She knew he was hiding in the pine barrens. Everyone spilled their guts when she told them he killed her son. Didn't matter if she sold out to The City then. No one could abide a child killer. And no one liked Billy, anyway. She and James were the only ones who ever protected him.

The pine barrens were thick, and you couldn't take a horse in. Maybe that was his reasoning, that he would have a better chance against her if they were both on foot. And maybe he was right. He had a *better* chance. But it still was bad.

Emma went to the pine barrens and found his tracks easily. No one went out there anymore, and Billy might have well just put up signs advertising where he went. Emma followed the tracks until nightfall, and then she waited, not sleeping, until early dawn, with the barest hint of twilight filling the air. She tracked him the rest of the way in the near dark.

Billy was smart enough not to light a fire, but that's all she gave him credit for. She found him sleeping on his bedroll in a little camp. He had laid out some traps around him, primitive snap traps, and some thicker branches and dry leaves, to give him warning.

Emma was a ghost and avoided them all. The sun was rising when she stood across from Billy in his small camp. He slept. He could sleep anywhere. She drew her pistol and aimed it at his head, right between his eyes. She could kill him now, but her rage wouldn't allow that.

It smoldered inside her. Her chest and lungs burned with it, a feeling she'd never felt before, born the moment she saw Thomas dead, a deep unsettling sense of incredible unfairness. Thomas was going to grow up big and strong and lead a civilized life in The City and Emma would leave behind something that wasn't death.

But it didn't happen. It was taken from her, by this man, and she stared at him, heat coming from her nostrils. Emma squeezed the grip of her pistol, her eyes aimed right where she needed.

"Wake up, Billy," she said. His eyes opened and spun to locate her, and his hand went to his pistol.

"Don't," she said. "Or I'll shoot you now."

He froze, and pulled his hand away from his gun, blinking his eyes awake, locating her.

"Can I sit up?"

"Sure," said Emma. "Go ahead."

Billy sat up, pushing himself off the ground, putting his back to a pine tree. He stared at her, his eyes wide. He looked terrified. Silence hung between them.

"I wasn't sure you'd come after me," he said, finally.

Emma stared daggers at him, her face emotionless, holding back the tide.

"You killed my boy, Billy," said Emma. "You think I'd just let it go?"

"I didn't know," said Billy. "I didn't know—"

"You didn't know you shot a child in the dark?" asked Emma. "Is that what you're telling me? You're telling me you didn't mean to kill the five-year-old kid?"

"I saw something in the dark, and I thought it was you or James—"

"How many fucking times did I tell you, Billy?" asked Emma, her eyes burning. "How many times did I tell you to not shoot at something you couldn't see?"

"You would have shot me—"

"We weren't armed, Billy!" said Emma. "The City took our guns, you fucking idiot! No guns inside the city limits. But you didn't think, not for a second. Just like always. And you shot a kid for nothing."

"No, not for nothing," said Billy. "The Rangers came for us, Emma." He stared at her, his impetuousness surfacing, daring her to shoot him. She wouldn't, not yet.

"That's what I figured would happen," said Emma.

"Lizzie, and Tom," said Billy. "They got shot in their saddles when they drew on them. Elijah, Steven, Marko—all taken. Probably to some work camp, out east somewhere. Heard they're expanding that way, too. Is that true? You were inside, for a long time. Figured you would know."

Emma didn't answer. "It was the price I paid—"

"Easy for you to pay it, huh, Emma?" asked Billy, almost shouting. "Easy for you to pay when it's somebody else's life. Harder to pay when it's your boy's."

Emma cocked her pistol.

"Go ahead," said Billy. "I know I ain't leaving alive. Shoot me. Get it over with."

"You deserve worse," said Emma.

"Deserve worse than being betrayed by the only people I ever trusted?" asked Billy. "Worse than being sold out so they could live a soft life under somebody else's thumb? You hear yourself? They didn't take your guns, Emma. You gave them up, willingly. They didn't strong-arm you. You did it of your own free will. When I killed your boy, it was an accident. I wanted to get you or James. Doubted I could do both, but I had to try. Never wanted to kill a kid. A mistake." He smiled, now. "But it wasn't an accident when you sold us out. We rode together for years, Emma. Years. And then you ran off to The City, and let them hunt us down like dogs. Forgot everything we built and burnt it down without a thought. And it wasn't no accident. You made a choice to hurt us all. Don't tell me about deserve. Because deserve don't have nothing to do with it."

Emma shot him BANG, the bullet hitting him right between the eyes. She shot him again, just to be sure.

"Do you really think this is going to change anything?"

Emma wavered, the monument still growing. Signs stood everywhere in the ruins, in the dark, ashy landscape she wandered through. Signs that read in many languages she couldn't understand, but several she could. Signs that read

Radiation exposure fatal at extended duration: TURN BACK NOW

Emma ignored them. Billy's voice snapped her eyes awake.

"Get out of here, Emma," said Billy. "You might still make it if you turn back. The City can fix you. Drop the body and run, if you can. Please."

"Please, please, please," said Emma. "You keep begging. Begging me to stop. To turn around. My boy didn't even get a chance—"

"Forgive him, Emma. It's your only chance. Let it go."

"Forgive him? What the hell are you talking about?"

"Billy," said the voice. "Forgive him. Leave him behind. Turn around. Go back to James. Get some help. Please."

"You're Billy," said Emma. "I'm carrying you to Hell, even if I burn alive. You won't trick me with some damn game.

I'm going to put you where you belong."

"Billy's dead, Emma. You killed him weeks ago. You bundled up his body, and tied him to your horse, and you rode west, and killed even more. Shot the only man you ever loved just so he couldn't save you."

"Shut your mouth, Billy," said Emma. "How many times—"

"I'm not Billy, Emma. This is your last chance. There's nothing out here but death. Thomas is dead. Billy is dead. And you will follow. You can turn around. You *can* still rebuild."

Emma stared up at the obelisk, a massive ugly stone thing that looked like a spire from Hell. It loomed over the land, and Emma could see them now, the rows and rows of graves in the distance. None of them marked. Hundreds and hundreds of them.

"I'm so close," said Emma. "All I have to do is bury you. A final judgment."

Billy didn't answer. The barren ground stretched out in front of her, the dark monument standing above her. A crack of lightning flashed in the distance. Massive stones littered the ground around her, each craggy and impregnable.

This proved it all, this terrible place, where you sent people to burn in Hell. People had argued it as superstition, as nonsense. Even Emma doubted, once upon a time. But now, seeing it, all those doubts disappeared. This was Hell, and Emma would put Billy into it.

"It's not what it appears, Emma. You're not thinking clearly. Please, stop."

Emma's body shook and trembled, her joints screaming with pain now. All her accrued injury and trauma burned through her, and her guts ached, her stomach roiling with nausea and agony. But the image of Thomas dead in Billy's arms ripped through her mind, and she kept walking, past the massive stony crags, past the warning signs, toward the massive stone monument, the marker for the gateway to Hell.

"I can't stop," she whispered as she walked. "I can't stop. He has to pay. I sacrificed everything for Thomas. Everything. With him gone, what's left?"

Her raspy voice bounced against the destruction.

"What's left?" she asked again. "What is there to turn back to?"

"You can rebuild your life, Emma."

Emma stared out over the tombs, over the Hellscape. Tears welled in her eyes, and she paused for a moment. But she dismissed her sadness, her fear, and let vengeance overtake them both. She would need it if she would finish this.

"It's too hard," she said, finally. "This is easier."

24

The graves were infinite.

They lined the slim path she walked. The black soil had been cleared of everything. All buildings, all plant life, anything that once stood on the soil was gone. Had the bombs done it?

Emma didn't know. The dark monument loomed large now, the sun almost completely set. The clouds didn't move here, a permanent home over the gateway to Hell. They swirled slowly above her, only shadow above them, only the barest sun filtering through.

It was enough light to see the row after row of graves, mounds of darkened dirt piled over thousands of bodies. Emma, with her hawk eyes, couldn't see the end of them spiraling off in every direction.

Emma felt liquid trickle from her nose and reached up to wipe it away. Her hand came back bloody, and every harsh breath burned. Something was in the air here, and Emma felt it sink into her lungs. Still, she walked.

There was no space for Billy, not anywhere, and she wouldn't risk burying him too far out. She walked closer to the monument, the massive thing growing larger and larger in her field of view. She trudged, her feet getting heavier with every step. They were filled with cement, and she felt her heels scrape the ground as she continued to walk. She reached for her canteen, but it was empty, and she dropped it with a *thunk*.

The light grew dimmer, but still she walked.

"Don't care how dark it is," said Emma. "I'll bury you, Billy. I'll dig in the dark if I have to. You'll pay. You'll pay."

Billy didn't answer, what remained of his corpse still strapped to her shoulders, and soon she would find his resting place, and she could drop her burden.

"Won't have to carry you around much longer, Billy," she said, her voice a croak. The monument grew larger and larger, and she thought she had to be close, and thought there would have to be an empty spot soon, but she saw nothing but filled graves. Emma craned her neck up, to see the top of the terrible stone tower, but then her feet hit something and she stumbled, and she fell.

She looked and saw it was a body, long dead.

No, not one body.

Two. It had been carrying the other in its arms. On their way to bury it. Both were mostly bones, the flesh long rotted away. Emma pushed herself up, her arms aching and trembling with effort. Her muscles didn't want to respond, but she pushed anyway, and she stood up, and saw the two bodies she had stumbled over weren't alone. More bodies littered the path. They had fallen on their way. But no body laid alone. All carried a second.

Emma walked past it, and kept her eyes on the corpses strewn on the path, avoiding each one, forcing her feet forward with every step. Her soles ached, and she felt liquid in her boots, and she realized she had lost her toenails. The pain had mixed with all her others, her body falling apart. She wouldn't make the mistake they made, though.

She would finish this. She walked.

The sun had set, and it was almost dark. Emma stopped and grabbed an arm from one corpse, and wrapped it in rags, dumping what remained of the little fuel she still carried in her bag. She lit it and held the torch forward. It would last until the end.

She approached the base of the monument, a massive concrete sculpture, the scope of which she finally understood. It loomed over her, hundreds of feet tall, an ugly thing with divots and sharpened points. She did not know who built it, or why, but it marked the center of the field, and she looked past it, and the calamity was worse beyond. More graves, for miles, and hundreds more dead, strewn across the ground, some near the graves, others in the path, and at this point it was hard to tell who had brought the dead here, and who had died in this place.

But she saw spaces now, places where she could finally bury Billy, and finish this, and mete out the justice he deserved.

"We're here, Billy," she said, stumbling over to an open space, past the corpses. "We're here. All of this, and finally, you'll get the punishment you deserve."

She stepped over other graves, to a space in the dark soil big enough for Billy's corpse. She planted her torch in the ground, and unstrapped him from her back, dropping him. Emma had expected the weight off her shoulders to feel good, but she barely felt a difference. Billy had weighed nearly nothing.

Emma stared at the dirt in front of her. She had no shovel, left behind at her horse.

She dropped to her knees and began scooping at the hard dark soil with her hands, plunging them into the dry, broken ground. The ground cracked beneath her fingers, even as her hands screamed with pain. Her fingernails came off in the earth, but it did not stop her, and she dug. She dug, and dug, throwing the soil to the side, on her hands and knees, her lungs filled with the scent of the poisoned land.

The dirt burned her skin, a pain that wouldn't stop, even when she pulled her hands away, and so she continued. She wouldn't stop now, not now, not after all she had done, all the blood she had spilled, all the suffering she had caused, she would finish this, she would bury Billy in this ground, and he would go to Hell for what he did. The dark monument laid there by God himself would condemn Billy to the inferno, and he would finally suffer an ounce of the pain she had felt when she saw her boy die in front of her, before he lived a fraction of his life, the child she had sacrificed everything for.

Everything she once believed, and everyone she once had cared for. She had condemned them all, her old gang first, and her own values, and even her true partner, her soul mate, who she had turned her back on, all because Billy had taken her boy from her, and he had to pay, had to pay the highest cost there was.

She dug and dug and dug until her hands were pink and raw and bloody, until the grave was deep enough. The torch burned in the dark and the black clouds swirled above her, but there was nothing else except for the monument to Hell, and she dug.

Emma stopped, her breath coming hard, in dark gory coughs, blood in her mouth. This was deep enough. She stood up, her back screaming, and she pulled Billy into the grave. The bundle slid inside, her blood all over it now. She bent over, her body wracked with coughs, the poisonous soil in her lungs, and every breath burned, but no, she had to finish, she had to cover him, those were the rules. A burial was a burial.

She forced herself up, even as she coughed, she couldn't stop coughing, and she pushed the pile of toxic soil over the body. Pounds and pounds of dirt went into the hole, over Billy, and Emma watched as he vanished.

Soon, the dirt covered him, a low mound that matched the hundreds and thousands of others clustered around the massive ugly monument.

"Goodbye, Billy," she coughed out.

Emma couldn't breathe, and she fell back onto the grave. She struggled to catch her breath, but it wouldn't come, no matter how hard she tried. There was something in the dirt, something in the dirt—

"You didn't have to do this," said a voice, out in the darkness.

"Who's—" started Emma, but her voice disappeared into a coughing fit.

A man walked into the sphere of light cast by her torch. He stepped over the other bodies and stood in front of her. He was dressed like James, even looked a little like him, but she couldn't place—

"It's Thomas, Mom," he said, his face full of gentle sadness.

"Oh—" she said, and coughed. She spit up a wad of flesh, and she could breathe, if only a little. "Oh, sweet Thomas." She felt a smile come to her face, her lips cracking.

"You came all the way out here," he said. "You shouldn't have."

"I did it for you," she said. "You were all I had."

Thomas kneeled next to her and took her hand in his. All Emma felt was agony, but suddenly her hand felt cool and free of pain.

"I know you did," said Thomas. "I know you did."

"You—" started Emma, swallowing blood. "You made everything I did worth it. All the pain. All the bad. You washed it away. And then he took you. He took you from me. He left me with only—" Emma coughed again.

"I'm here now," he said. "For you."

Emma squeezed his hand, and he smiled at her. He looked so much like James. He'd grow up so strong.

"I can't—" started Emma, closing her eyes, letting go of his hand. She couldn't lift her arms. They were so heavy. Everything was so heavy. Everything was dark. She felt Thomas's touch.

It was a small comfort.

About the Author

Robbie Dorman believes in horror. Burial is his tenth novel. When not writing, he's podcasting, playing video games, or petting cats. He lives in Texas with his wife, Kim.

You can follow Robbie on Twitter @robbiedorman

Acknowledgements

Thank you to my wife Kim, for her patience and support. Thank you to my team of beta readers; Andrew, Matt, Megan, and Yousef, for your guidance and help. Thank you, for reading.

Sign up for TWO free, exclusive novels!

Sign up for Robbie's newsletter! Monthly sneak peeks at upcoming projects, cover teases, and instant access to TWO FREE, EXCLUSIVE novels!

www.robbiedorman.com/newsletter